GEORGE TAKES A STAND

"And you want to know something else?" I said. "I'm not going to college at all next year. Not even the University of Minnesota."

Dad slowly got to his feet, as though he didn't quite trust himself not to rush me. "Okay, you've said it," he said. "You're my son, and I'm responsible for your food, shelter, and medical care, but beyond that, you're on your own. You want to live your life without any help from me, you've got it. Anything you want besides the mere necessities, you buy for yourself. Is that understood?"

"Yes," I said, my heart still pounding. "Understood."

PHYLLIS REYNOLDS NAYLOR is the Newbery award-winning author of *Shiloh* and has written more than fifty books for both children and adults. She lives in Maryland with her husband and two grown sons.

THE
YEAR
OF THE
GOPHER

PHYLLIS
REYNOLDS
NAYLOR

LAUREL-LEAF BOOKS

Published by
Dell Publishing
a division of
Bantam Doubleday Dell Publishing Group, Inc.
1540 Broadway
New York, New York 10036

Excerpts from THE INSIDER'S GUIDE TO THE COLLEGES, 1981–82: Compiled and Edited by the staff of "The Yale Daily News" © 1981 reprinted by permission of the publisher, G. P. Putnam's Sons (A Perigee Book)

ISBN: 0-440-21591-9

RL: 5.9

Reprinted by arrangement with Atheneum–Macmillan Publishing Company

Printed in the United States of America

June 1993

10 9 8 7 6 5 4 3

OPM

To the men in my life—
R., J., and M.—
and to Julie,
the newest member of our family,
with love

ONE

At twelve, the sun reached the *Touch of Silk* calendar on my wall; it shone on the legs of the girl in the picture as though she were tanning only half her body. By twelve thirty-three it had touched the tip of my boomerang, and five minutes later it was fading the photo of Karen Gunderson. There were thumbtack holes in Karen Gunderson's picture where I'd decided, once, to give her acne. Karen Gunderson never had a pimple in her life.

I scratched my stomach and let one foot hang over the edge of the mattress. If Mom didn't yell pretty soon, I was going to waste the whole day. The window was open, and the dry yellow leaves of the box elder scraped against the screen. I could hear a portable radio on the steps outside, then the postman wrestling with the mail slot.

Kerplunk. Downstairs, something hit the slate floor of the foyer.

Dartmouth, I told myself.

Kerplunk again.

Princeton. I rolled over and tunneled beneath

the pillow. Those were the only two catalogs yet to come.

"George!" Mom called. "You just got Princeton and Dartmouth. Get up, or you'll waste the whole day."

Name:	Richards,	George	T.
	(Last)	*(First)*	*(Middle Initial)*
Address:	5181 Clarion Place		
	Minneapolis, Minnesota		
Age:	17		
Hobbies:			

I sat mauling a muffin at the kitchen table while I studied one of my college application forms. I'd taken the whole stack downstairs and piled them next to my plate. Mom looked over my shoulder every time she passed. I could feel her breathing on my hair.

"Colleges love to see lots of hobbies," she said. "You could list photography, music, swimming, stamp collecting. . . ."

"Mom, I don't collect stamps."

"Remember how you saved those envelopes Aunt Donna sent us?"

"Because they were from England," I told her.

"Well, it looks good to have a collection of something," Mom said.

I brightened. "Beer cans! Back in sixth grade, Bud Irving and I collected fifteen sacks. I've still got the Hapsburg and 007."

Now Mom was getting angry. We've both got green eyes that look brown when we're mad. Same snubby kind of nose, same square jaw. . . .

"Use your head," Mom told me, which she says every other day, at least.

Ollie came in for lunch. On weekends, he eats lunch about the time I'm having breakfast. Ollie's twelve, and he'll never know how many times I've saved his life. Like last year when he needed glasses and Dad was about to get him a pair of horn rims. I talked him into contact lenses instead. No kid wants to go through life looking like an owl, especially if his name is Oliver. The year before that, Mom was all ready to enroll him in that private school where she teaches. I told her that if she took Ollie away from his friends and put him in that school for wealthy snots, he'd start wetting his bed or something. She must have believed me because she let him stay at Parkhurst Elementary.

I gave Ollie one of my sausages to hold him while Mom fixed his hamburger.

"You going to weight-lift today, George?" Ollie asked me, stuffing the sausage in his mouth sideways. All the repulsive things I used to do, Oliver does now, but it doesn't bother me one bit.

"Yeah. Going over to Psycho's and use the bench press," I said.

"I *wish* you wouldn't call Marshall that," Mom said, rummaging through the lid drawer. "Mrs. Evans would have a stroke if she knew you called him Psycho."

Ollie grinned at me across the table.

"Just a nickname, Mom," I told her.

"But Marshall's such a gentle person, really."

I laughed out loud. "That's the joke! He's a great big lovable hunk, so we call him Psycho." I took a bite of toast and went on chewing. I wasn't about to tell Mom that Marsh got his nickname because he'd started throwing packages of sandwich buns around the 7-Eleven one night after too much beer. Or that we called Bud Irving "Discount" because he'd been fired the summer before from Fotomat for giving discounts to his friends.

"I want to go to Psycho's and lift," said Ollie.

"Can't," I told him. "Stunt your growth."

"You're putting me on."

"No, I heard that somewhere," I said. "Shouldn't start heavy lifting till you're past puberty. You can use my dumbbells in the basement, though, if you want."

I took the applications back up to my room and sprawled on my bed, leafing through them all. *Why did you choose this University?* asked one. (A blank page followed, good for about 500 words.) *How, in your opinion, does college life mirror the world at large?* asked a second. (Another blank page.) *If, in your choice of careers, you could help alleviate one of mankind's most pressing problems, which problem would that be, and why? Attach to this page an essay of approximately 700 words describing a situation in which you successfully faced a challenge.*

I was back down in the kitchen five minutes later for the cheese crackers.

"You can't even have started!" Mom said. She had a box of photos on the table and was looking for a picture of me to send to Princeton. Most of them had been taken when I was in junior high, and I looked like a nerd.

"I've got till December," I told her, and went on out in the yard where Typhus, our old setter, was drooling on the patio. She was a stray when Ollie found her, and looked so awful that Dad called her Typhoid Mary. "Typhus" was the name that stuck. I gave her a cheese cracker.

It wasn't "mankind's most pressing problem" that was putting me off or even the 700-word essay. I wasn't sure *what* I was feeling except that it seemed to go back a long, long way—as though my parents had put me on a train ten years ago and I couldn't get off. Couldn't even see out the windows. It went racing down the same track where Trish had gone before me— where Jeri and Oliver were supposed to come after. I mean, if you don't know where you're going, you won't know if you're halfway to the place you're supposed to be, if you get what I mean. I tried to explain this to Dad once, but he didn't understand.

"You need a good education," he told me, "because, A: you want to be a well-informed citizen; B: you want to take your rightful place in society; and C: you'll need a job." Dad's a lawyer, and he has this tendency to outline.

A: I didn't have the slightest idea of what I wanted to do with my life, so how did I know I needed a college education to do it?

B: I wasn't sure I'd like college.

C: I wasn't even sure I could make it through. Trish hadn't made it through yet. Trish went to Cornell, and in her sophomore year, the invitations went out:

Mr. and Mrs. Phillip Edgar Richards

cordially invite you

to the marriage of their daughter

Patricia Claire

to

Roger Blake Trenton III. . . .

Trish wanted to leave college and get a job until Roger got through graduate school, but Mom and Dad wouldn't hear of it, said they'd help out financially if Trish would just get her degree.

"That's the trouble with falling in love," Dad said as we stood behind the stephanotis at the reception. "Never happens at the right time. It's up to you now, son. Set an example for Jeri and Oliver. Show them how it's done—how you've got to put your mind to something and see it through."

I realized I had just fed Typhus the entire box of cheese crackers. She slunk off the edge of the patio, stuck her head in the mums, and threw up.

"George," Mom was calling. "Come help me decide which photo should go to Princeton and which one to Dartmouth."

I went inside and walked on by her.

"I've got till December," I said again, and went back upstairs.

Psycho's room took up half the Evans' basement. His brothers were all grown up and had moved out, so any furniture his mom didn't want found its way into Psycho's space. He had a double bed, a single bed, a black-and-white TV, an old leather recliner, and traffic signs on the walls. FRONT END PARKING ONLY, it said above his bed.

Both his parents were tall and skinny. Marsh was tall, too, but he weighed about 185. You see him coming down a dark alley, you'd turn around and go back. Only thing Psycho ever attacked, though, was a mayfly. He just swatted it with his big paw and then held it up by one wing and studied it sorrowfully, like maybe he shouldn't have done it.

The three of us—Psycho, Discount, and I—got together about three times a week to work out. Marsh and I were serious about it—had a program set up and everything. Bud Irving just did what the spirit moved him to do.

There had been twin daughters in the Irving family before Bud came along, and they both died a week after they were born. So Discount got anything he wanted. Computer? You got it. Component stereo? Seven-piece Ludwig drum set? Sure, Bud. We'll run right out tomorrow and get it for you. When it came time for Discount to have a car, we told him to ask for a Porsche, but he just laughed. His folks gave him a used Datsun 280Z instead, which was nicer than the cars Psycho and I drove. Life was too easy for Bud Irving. So when it came to working out, Bud talked more than he lifted. Me? I simply wanted to be huge. I mean, when it was prom time, I wanted to go in a 17-inch collar. Already I could see my trapezoids getting massive.

When I got to Psycho's, he was already benching, Discount spotting him, so I grabbed the dumbbells and started doing my curls. Psycho had on a pair of purple boxers that stuck out beneath his gym shorts. I started to make a joke, then kept quiet. You don't go for laughs when a guy's lifting. Both Bud and I were a long way from what Psycho could do on the bench press. When Psycho lifted, every weight in the place was on the bar.

"What are you doing this time?" I asked him as we changed places. "Twelve, twelve, twelve?" Psycho does his repeats on the bench press in batches.

"Naw—twelve, ten, eight," Marsh said, his thighs like Virginia hams, as he slid off.

I was lying there, breathing hard, my hands in their leather gloves locked round the bar, getting ready for the lift, when Discount said, "Know what I heard yesterday? Karen Gunderson's on the Pill."

I relaxed my grip and looked at Bud. He had on a T-shirt that said, IF IT MOVES, FONDLE IT.

"How do you know?" I asked him.

"Jake told me. He's a cashier at Walgreen's. Karen came in to pick up a prescription and there it was, right on the sack—Ovulen, or something. Jake said she turned all shades of red when he handed it to her."

"So he's going around school telling everyone?"

"Only stating the facts." Discount grinned.

"Why doesn't he just take out an ad in the paper?" I said. Then I gripped the bar hard and hoisted the weights, and when Discount put out one hand to help me, like maybe I couldn't get it up, I growled at him to back off.

I don't know what I was mad about, exactly.

Karen had been going with some guy named Bob Ellis for about a year, and you never saw them together that they weren't touching. It's just that Karen was about the most gorgeous girl in Minneapolis, and there probably wasn't a guy in school who hadn't imagined how she looked in the raw. Maybe each of us secretly dreamed about being the first to sleep with Karen, but now that we knew officially she was on the pill, it ruined the fantasy. And maybe I was still angry because I'd had a crush on her back in my freshman year, and she hadn't even known I was around.

"Ellis sure is lucky," said Psycho, and there was a wistful tone to his voice. The only girl Psycho had been out with was his cousin. The three of us—Marsh, Bud, and I—were talking once about how we'd spend our time if we only had one day left to live. St. Francis of Assisi said that if he knew he were to die tomorrow, he'd go on hoeing his garden. What the three of *us* said was that we'd make out with Karen Gunderson. So much for being noble.

At that moment, though, I wasn't imagining Karen in the raw. I was imagining her facing Jake Perona there at the prescription counter and turning red. Some girls wouldn't care how many people knew they were on the pill. One girl in Algebra II even told me herself. But Karen would care. I could just see the sly smile on Jake's face when he handed her the pills, see his eyes dance. If it had been me at the prescription counter, I would have picked up that sack without hardly even looking at it, then rung up the price—sort of a reflex action, you know. I'd ask her something about school while I stapled the sack shut, and I imagined how she'd appreciate it. Somehow she'd know that I wasn't going to let on that I knew, least of all tell anybody, and she'd be grateful forever.

"Hey, George, you going to lift or just lie there looking at it?" Discount said. I realized I'd stopped again. I gripped the bar, remembering to breathe out on the thrust, shoved the weights overhead, held them a second, then let my elbows bend. The bar bounced slightly in my hands as I lowered it toward my chest. Eight times, nine, ten. . . .

At dinner that evening, I'd barely buttered my potato when Mom said to Dad, "The Princeton catalog came today. So did Dartmouth."

"That's all of them, then." Dad beamed at me. "Well, George, looks like you've got your work cut out for you. You keep track of all the deadlines now, and get those applications in on time."

Jeri and I both reached for the catsup. She got there first and one of her nails scratched my thumb. Jeri's fifteen and looks like me, and we both resemble Mom. Ollie and Trish look like my father, with dark hair and thin noses and long necks, like swans or something.

"I don't know, Dad," I heard myself saying. "Not much point in going to college if I haven't figured out yet what I want to do."

"That's the whole idea of college," Dad told me. "First you go and then you decide what you'll major in."

"How long did it take you to find out you wanted to be a lawyer?"

"Knew it as far back as fourth grade," Dad said, which didn't exactly help.

Jeri had on headphones under her long sandy

hair, and she sat drumming her fingers on the table as she ate.

"Take those off, *please*?" Mom begged in exasperation. "Couldn't we for once have ordinary table conversation like an ordinary, everyday family?"

Jeri took off the headphones and dropped them under her chair along with her Walkman. She picked up her fork in a gesture of great disgust and slid a bite of food into her mouth, using only her teeth, as though she couldn't bear to let her lips touch it.

Dad turned again to me: "The thing you've got to remember is that you're going to be spending eight hours a day at a job for the rest of your life, so you'd better choose it carefully."

That didn't help much either.

"All you do," Dad continued, leaning his elbows on the table, "is figure out all the things you like to do—things you do best—put them together, and see what you come up with."

I thought it over while I ate my peas. Maybe deciding what I wanted to be was simpler than I'd imagined. I liked animals—Typhus, especially; I liked weight-lifting; I liked fooling around in a combo, with Discount on the drums.

"I've got it!" I said, suddenly. "A two-hundred-pound veterinarian who plays the saxophone."

Dad didn't think it particularly funny.

TWO

On weekends, if there was anything doing, I worked as a parking attendant for Saunders Funeral Home. "Anything doing" meant if somebody had died. I felt like a vulture when I called in on Friday to see if they'd need me.

What I did was set up chairs for the memorial service and then go outside. If the lot in back was full and people were parking along the driveway, I'd ask them to leave their keys and, if I was lucky, I'd get to move a Mercedes now and then.

I hadn't had the job long, but already I'd discovered that a funeral home's a good place to do your heavy thinking. I mean, no one kidded around with you when you were standing outside Saunders in a suit and tie, looking sober. Guys would drive by without even honking, like it was a hospital zone or something.

I thought about things like how come it's someone else who's there in the coffin and I'm the one who's alive? Why are "acts of God" always something horrible, floods and hurricanes and stuff? How come you can step outside and get struck by a bolt of lightning, but you're never hit with a free trip to Europe? I mean, if God is great, God is good, how come the only surprise we ever get is water in the basement?

I mentioned this once to Dad.

He studied me a good long while and then said, "You know something, George? You're one out of four hundred million. Four hundred million spermatazoa were racing for the ovum, and you're the one who got there first. Four hundred million other kids I could have had, and look what I got."

We'd laughed, but I'll admit, it gave me pause.

On this particular evening, though, I wasn't thinking about God, I was thinking about Dad. About how it wasn't what he said so much, it was what he meant. I could tell by his face at dinner that he was worried I really *might* become a veterinarian or something equally unacceptable. I knew that if I'd asked what was wrong with being a vet, he would have said, "Nothing at all, George! Medicine's a fine occupation! But what have you got against people?" Which is why I let it slide.

The month before, for example, when he named all the universities I should apply to, they were Ivy League, all the way. He practically recited them in alphabetical order! When I said, "What's wrong with the University of Minnesota?" he said, "Nothing, George! It's an excellent school. But what have you got against the others?"

I couldn't help thinking that beneath all that free choice I was supposed to have was the old railroad. The engine was fired up and the seat was reserved, but it didn't really matter where I wanted to get off because the train wasn't stopping till the end of the line, and it was Dad who bought my ticket.

It wasn't just Dad, though. Mom always wanted

to know why we couldn't have normal conversations at the table like an ordinary family, but she didn't really want us to be ordinary at all. "Ordinary" scared the heck out of her. Any time we showed the slightest interest in something academic, Mom was looking ahead to our Ph.D.'s. I remember once when I was nine, and a kid showed me how you could make your own erupting volcano by pouring vinegar on a little baking soda. Mom found me out on the sidewalk with the bicarbonate of soda and the vinegar bottle, and the next day she presented me with a $29 chemistry set. The first time Trish came home with her notebook covered with doodles, Mom goes out and gets her a sketch pad, charcoal, and a few pastels. All you had to do in our house was hum, and you were signed up for music lessons. Jeri, in fact, made the mistake of asking the difference between a viola and a violin, and got six years of piano. It wasn't that our parents *cared* that bothered us—bothered me, anyway; it was what they cared *about*.

Dave Hahn came around the side of the funeral home. He was seventeen, too, and worked the same shift, back lot. It was Dave who had recommended me for the job. He'd only been with Saunders a couple of months himself, but already he spoke the lingo. People who drown in the lakes, for example, were "floaters"; bodies that had been dead awhile were "decomps". This time Dave was carrying a bunch of white mums and yellow roses, and he handed it to me.

"For your girlfriend," he said.

"What are you talking about?" I asked him.

"Saunders doesn't care," he said. "We've got

five bouquets back in the shed; I'm going to drive them to a hospital later. Some guy was cremated this morning, so we give his flowers away after. You want pink instead? Whole lot of pink out there."

"Jeez, Dave!" I said, and shoved the flowers back in his hand. "I can't give a girl flowers from a funeral home!"

Dave just shrugged. "Flowers are flowers. I'd give 'em to Sue, but she only goes for the red ones." As music came from inside, signaling the end of the service, Dave took the flowers down to the end of the drive and propped them beneath a bush, and after a while a dog came along and peed on them.

My sociology teacher said once that all pretty girls ought to experience one month of their lives being ugly, just to know how it feels. I was thinking about that on Monday, sitting a couple rows away from Karen Gunderson in history class. Karen was wearing designer jeans and a bluish sweater with puffy knobs of wool along the shoulders. Her hair, sort of beige-blond, was long and curled under at the edges. She had the kind of body you'd see in a Coppertone ad.

While Mrs. Hartman, up front, discussed the Italian Renaissance, I was thinking how my sociology teacher had said that each of us has two selves—the one you see on the outside and the self within—and that if we were blind, we might think of the most gorgeous girl in class as ugly, and the ugliest girl, because of her inner charm, beautiful.

Of course, there are some girls, like Karen Gunderson, who have it all—looks, charm, personality. . . . I tried to focus on her personality, but my eyes kept dropping to her thighs and the way her jeans fit snug—the way her feet looked inside her sandals, with shell-pink polish on her toenails. And then, too late, I realized that something was going on with Karen that I hadn't even noticed; about half a dozen other guys were looking at her, too.

I watched as Karen pulled her feet back under her desk, as though the less anyone could see of her, the better. She was making little marks all up and down one side of her notebook. They were angry-looking marks, like stairsteps, getting wider and darker as they traveled up the page. When I glanced at her face, she never even lifted her eyes. Her cheeks were flaming, the way you look when you have a fever.

Some guy on the other side of her caught my eye and grinned. Then I knew that practically everyone in the room, Mrs. Hartman excluded, had heard about Karen's prescription for Ovulen —that Jake had spread it around the school.

I wanted to tell Karen that Jake was a jerk. I decided that the best thing I could do, though, was quit looking at her. So I folded my arms across my chest and tried to concentrate on the revival of the heliocentric theory that Mrs. Hartman was so excited about.

When the bell rang, Karen grabbed her books and stood up, but the notebook slipped out of her arms and hit the floor. The rings sprung open and her papers spilled out into the aisle.

"Here," I said, scooping up a handful.

"Thanks," she murmured. She stuffed them inside the cover and fled the room.

I was on my way to physics when I felt two fingers poking the small of my back. A girl's voice said, "Gotcha!" Reaching around, I grabbed Maureen Kimball's hand and heard her laugh. She moved up beside me and latched onto my arm.

"How you doing?" I asked.

She made a face. Her face is already tiny, and when she wrinkles it up, the features all run together—a squished-up little face topped by red hair. "Just made a mess of a psych test," she said. "There goes my B average."

Maureen's fingers sort of kneaded my arm, like she was searching for something under my sleeve. I flexed my biceps just a little, not so much that she'd notice.

"Going to the game this Saturday?" she asked.

I knew if I said yes, she'd want me to go with her. "I don't know," I stalled. "I may have to work on that English paper."

"Do it Sunday," she said.

"I'll see," I told her, and gave her a little tap as we reached the corner. She went on down the hall to orchestra.

Maureen Kimball has had a crush on me since we were in seventh grade. She never gives up. Sometimes I think if she'd stop chasing me, I could get interested. How come the girls you like fall for someone else and the girls you don't care much about fall for you?

I'd never actually been in love—I mean the kind of thing where you're both crazy about each other. Discount said he was once, but it hadn't happened to me yet. I figured it must be pretty special, though. I remember when Trish got engaged. This was the girl who got an art scholarship and was going to study sculpture. When she left for college, she said that her career was the most important thing in her life. The next year, though, she brought Roger Blake Trenton III home with her at Christmas, and I guess he gave her a ring on Christmas Eve, because she woke us all up about midnight to tell us she was *engaged, engaged, engaged!* to be *married, married, married!* And the next morning everybody was so interested in Trish and how she wasn't going to be around much longer that Ollie got away with murder. He ate half a box of chocolates before breakfast and opened at least five presents that weren't even his.

It wasn't till Christmas was over that I suddenly felt sorry for Jeri. Only for a moment, but sorry. It was like she wasn't even around. Trish and Roger went to church Christmas Day with our family, and Trish was showing everyone her ring. The Wonder Girl of the family. First she gets herself a scholarship to a prestigious college and then she gets herself a man with a Roman numeral after his name. For just a moment I caught a look of envy in Jeri's eyes—panic, almost. Trish was a hard act to follow. I felt like going over to Jeri and saying that it really wasn't such a big deal. But I didn't.

When I got home, I found an article Dad had clipped out of the business section and left strategically placed on the kitchen table. It showed the various incomes of different occupations, and lawyers were right up there near the top along with neurosurgeons. Considerably further down were veterinarians, with musicians somewhere near the bottom. Dad had put a check mark beside all three. *Just thought you'd find this interesting,* he had scribbled along one side.

I left the article where it was and got some lunch meat and a can of Sprite out of the refrigerator. Typhus followed me into the living room, her tail flopping from side to side like a dust mop. I tore off a slice for her as I opened my books and started a review for a physics quiz.

Jeri came home a little later. She went right to the stereo and turned it on, then went out to the kitchen and yelled because I'd taken the last Sprite.

The truth is that Jeri and I didn't get along. We never did. Mom thought it was because we're only two years apart. I really couldn't explain it myself, because I got on all right with Trish when she was there, and I loved Ollie, but I'd look at Jeri and realize she was going to be aunt to my kids some day, and then I'd start feeling sorry for my kids.

Once, in fact, I felt so guilty about how badly Jeri and I got along that for a whole week I pretended she was dying and that each day might be the last I'd see her again. It worked for a while, but by the fourth day I felt like hurrying her along.

She came out of the kitchen carrying the newspaper clipping. "What's this?" she asked.

"Something Dad put out for me to read," I told her, and hunkered down further on the sofa with my physics book so she'd know I didn't want to be disturbed.

"That's a laugh—you a vet," Jeri said, and sprawled on the chair across from me.

I didn't even look up. "I'm not going to be a vet," I said evenly.

She ignored it. "Every pet you ever had died. You'd get hit with a malpractice suit the very first week."

"Will you shut up? I'm trying to study," I snapped.

Jeri didn't shut up. "Hamster, goldfish, cat . . . *two* cats. . . ." she said, counting on her fingers. "One parakeet, a turtle. . . ." She named all the pets she could remember, even the ones that died of old age, even the pets that belonged to someone else. "Poor Typhus," Jeri told the dog.

I tried not to listen—pretended she wasn't there. Jeri got up finally and turned the stereo even louder.

THREE

During the big Oktoberfest in Milwaukee, Dave Hahn drove down with a couple of friends and came back with a moon tattoo on his backside. It's on his left hip, about six inches below the belt-line. He showed it to us during gym.

Mom found out about it when Dave "mooned" a bunch of girls at the bus stop, and one of them was Jeri. She thought it was a riot. She told Mom how Dave lowered his jeans and bent over, and how the girls all screamed and laughed. Mom didn't scream, but she didn't laugh, either.

"Isn't that about what you'd expect from Dave Hahn?" she said, and went on grading the papers she had spread out over the dining room table.

I decided not to get mixed up in that one, and went on upstairs.

I've known Dave since I was eleven. He lives down the street in a redwood house, but I've never been inside it. Shortly after I got to know him back in sixth grade, Mom sat me down and told me that I could have Dave over any time I liked, but she thought it best that I not go there, because his dad had a friend.

It was one of those situations where you know

your mom is very politely telling you something awful. I couldn't figure what the heck she was getting at.

"It's a male friend," Mom had said, and then she'd told me that Mr. Hahn was gay. Only she didn't say "gay," she said "homosexual." Then, before I could ask how he could be Dave's father if he was homosexual, she said, well, actually, Mr. Hahn was bisexual, but he preferred males. And *she* would prefer that I stay away from the redwood house.

I remember that I hadn't known what to say; both Mom and I sort of stared at the rug.

"You mean I can't *ever* go there?" I'd asked finally.

"Well, not for a while," she said. "Not until you've worked through your own sexual identity."

That one really threw me.

At the same time Mom was laying down rules for me, the other moms must have been doing the same, because after Dave invited me to his house a few times and I made excuses, he quit asking. He stopped asking the other guys, too. When we all went out together, Dave would just meet us somewhere. In the six years I'd known Dave, he never talked about it, and neither did we.

I'd see him and his dad at the movies sometimes, and Mr. Hahn looked like anybody else's dad—just a square-built guy with a bald spot on the back of his head.

Anyway, two weeks after Dave came back from Milwaukee with his moon tattoo, the four of us —Dave, Psycho, Discount, and I—went to a party, and Dave had a few beers. Psycho and Discount, too. I didn't have any because I was driving.

The girl's parents came home and found twice as many people as they'd expected, so the party broke up early. We got back in the car and went cruising around, trying to decide whether to go bowling or drive up to Burger King. I guess Dave Hahn had had more than a few beers, because he sat there in the back seat laughing at everything as though he couldn't stop—like when you get hiccups or something.

"Did you see Lisa's mother when she found kids roaming around upstairs?" Psycho said, and he imitated the high-pitched voice of Lisa's mother: "Henry, there are *boys* in the *bedrooms! Do* something!"

Dave was off again. He was laughing so hard that it turned into little wheezing noises.

"You okay, Dave?" Discount asked him.

I turned around at the next light. Dave's shoulders shook convulsively, and tears ran down his cheeks.

"Is he laughing or crying?" I asked.

A huge guffaw erupted from Dave's mouth, and then he bent over double.

"Dave," Discount said, "how many beers did you have?"

Dave managed to hold up the fingers on both hands.

"Jeez!" I said, taking off again. "We've got to sober this dude up before we take him home."

We drove around for another half-hour, and just as we passed a pet store in a shopping center, I heard Dave say, "I wanna rabbit."

"It's closed, Dave," I said, "and you need a rabbit like you need a virus."

Dave was off again, wheezing and choking, and

23

the rest of us were laughing at him, but then he got serious. Dave drunk and serious was even worse than Dave drunk and hysterical.

"I wanna *rabbit!*" he yelled. "I *always* wanted a rabbit!"

Psycho offered Dave one of his goldfish—*two* goldfish—if he'd just shut up, but Dave was getting angry. He started to bellow and pounded his fists against the back of the front seat.

"Cut it out, Dave," I told him.

"I wanna *rabbit!*" he bellowed. "Dammit, George, you better let me out."

"The store's *closed,* Dave, for Pete's sake!"

We had just come to a stoplight and I could see the elderly couple in the car next to us look over disapprovingly. I wished it wasn't so bright there under the street lamps—that we were invisible somehow.

Suddenly I heard Discount yell, "*No,* Dave!" But it was too late.

I turned around in time to see Dave up on the seat, his rear end toward the window, his pants down, mooning the elderly couple in the blue Pontiac.

I didn't even wait for the light. I took off as Discount was wrestling Dave down off the seat. I turned a corner and then another. We had just passed the Holy Angels Academy on Nicollet when I saw a red light flashing in my rearview mirror.

"Oh, no!" I breathed. Psycho saw it, too.

"Dave!" he said, whirling around. "Shut up! Just shut up! We've got a squad car behind us!"

Carefully, I pulled over to the curb and stopped. I was afraid Dave would moon the police. He'd quit bellowing, though, and was sitting up straight, hands on his knees. Discount had hold of his collar. I rolled down the window as an officer came up alongside the car.

"Good evening," said the officer. He had a flashlight and shone it through the window, first on Psycho, who sat like a dazed frog beside me, then on Discount and Dave in the backseat.

"Was I speeding?" I asked.

"No," the policeman said, "but we got a report that someone in this car exposed himself to a couple in a blue Pontiac." He shone the flashlight in the backseat again. I looked around. Both Discount and Dave were staring straight ahead. "Someone," the officer said, "with a tattoo on his behind. Now I wonder which one of you fellas that might be."

Psycho went rigid on the seat beside me. I was afraid the officer was going to make us all line up outside and drop our pants.

The officer leaned a little farther in the window and I knew he was trying to get a whiff of my breath.

"License?" he said.

I pulled out my wallet. Dave was giggling softly again. I could hear Discount pleading with him to shut up.

The policeman looked at my license. "Anybody in this car twenty-one?" he asked.

"No, sir," I said.

"*Nobody* in this car twenty-one? All you guys been drinking?"

"Not me," I said. Man, oh, man, was I glad I hadn't had even one beer back at the party.

Dave's laugh was getting louder. He'd shut up for about five seconds, then cut loose again.

"Problem, here, with your friend?" the officer said.

"He wants a rabbit," Discount told him.

The officer looked inside again. "What?"

"He's had a few beers, officer," I said. "We were just driving him around awhile before we took him home."

"I see," said the policeman. This time he looked right at me. "I'd like you fellas to follow me in to the police station. Next left, then a right."

He went on back to his cruiser.

Psycho moaned again.

"You see what you've done, you ass?" Discount was saying to Dave, shaking him hard. "Shut *up!* Just shut *up!*"

"What do you think they'll do to us?" Psycho asked as I waited till the squad car pulled alongside me.

"I don't know," I said, turning the key in the ignition. My lips felt dry. "If they jail Dave, have we got enough money for bail?"

"I got four dollars," said Discount from the backseat.

Dave was hysterical again. Each wheezing burst of laughter seemed to trigger another.

By the time we got to the station, though, and stopped, he was all laughed out. Discount pulled him out of the car, and Dave stood there unsteadily on the asphalt, blinking up at the arc lights. Then he looked at the policeman over by the walk and blinked some more.

"What you got?" the desk sergeant asked as we all came through the door.

"Indecent exposure," the officer said.

The desk sergeant looked us over. "All four of them?"

"Just one. He was mooning from the rear window of a car."

The desk sergeant sighed wearily. "Give me your phone numbers," he said.

We sat on a wooden bench against one wall while we waited for our dads to come get us. There wasn't any charge; we simply were not allowed to leave until our parents got there. The humiliation factor, or something.

Reality was finally sinking in on Dave.

"Dad'll kill me," he mumbled as we watched the hand on the clock move from midnight to ten after.

I leaned back and tried to imagine the scenario at my house. Mom always talks about that "call in the night" that she's been expecting ever since Trish started to date. Anytime Trish was out and the phone rang after ten o'clock, Mom expected the State Highway Patrol at the very least. The worst thing that happened with Trish was a flat tire over in St. Paul, and Dad had to go change it. I could just see Mom stumbling across the bedroom now to answer the phone, hear her voice as she said, "Phil! It's the police!" I figured Dad would probably get up and put on a suit and tie. Lawyers never go anyplace without a suit and tie. Maybe, because it was the police, he'd even put on a vest.

Dad wasn't without humor. He used to sit up with me occasionally to watch David Letterman or *Saturday Night Live*, and when Letterman put on his Velcro suit or jumped in a tank of water wearing sponges, Dad laughed as hard as I did. It just seemed that the closer I got to graduation and college, the more tense Dad became, as though to impress on me that the time for silliness was over, and the real world was waiting. He wouldn't see anything funny, I knew, in this little escapade.

It was Dave's dad who got there first. He was wearing an old pair of jeans, loafers without any socks, and a hunting jacket. His beard was starting to show. He stepped inside the door, looked at us, and finally said, in a sad kind of voice, "Dave, what happened?"

That's what really gets to you. I knew that all of us had been sitting there figuring out what to say when our folks stormed in raising hell. We weren't prepared for sympathy or understanding. Dave sort of crumbled. He just sat there with his eyes down, his lips quivering, like he had back in sixth grade when the science teacher caught him throwing toilet paper wads at the ceiling. Mr. Hahn turned toward the desk sergeant.

"Indecent exposure," the sergeant said, and looked bored.

Dave's father stared at the rest of us.

"He mooned someone in another car," I explained.

Mr. Hahn turned back to Dave again. "That all you can find to do on a Saturday night?" he asked. And when Dave still didn't answer, he said, "Come on, let's go home." He turned to the officer who was sitting at the end of our bench. "I'm sorry for any trouble he caused you."

"So am I," the officer said. "I've got better things to do."

Mr. Irving and Mr. Evans came in the door together. Evans was mad.

"Marsh, what the hell . . . ?" he said.

"I didn't do anything," Psycho told him.

"Then how come you're sitting here?" his father exploded.

"We make it a policy to call the parents when we bring in minors," the desk sergeant explained. "We catch a carload of boys mooning, we bring 'em all in."

"Doing *what*?" Marshall's father asked, and we had to explain it to him. He and Mr. Irving both looked at us like we were crazy. Then Dad came in.

He wasn't wearing a tie. He had on a white shirt, all right, but it was unbuttoned at the collar and one side of his face still had a pillow crease on it. We had to explain all over again about mooning. I don't think I ever felt so ridiculous.

I couldn't tell what Dad was thinking. He didn't look mad; didn't look worried, particularly. I guess you could say he was dazed.

"Is there a charge against my son?" he asked the desk sergeant.

The officer shook his head, and Dad thanked him very much.

Dave and his father were still standing by their car talking when we came out. None of the dads said anything to Mr. Hahn. They didn't say much to each other, either. I got back in my own car. Psycho and Discount got in their dads' cars.

I drove down Nicollet to 46th and then over to

Clarion Place, with Dave and his dad in the lead, my dad behind me, Psycho's dad and Mr. Irving bringing up the rear; a four-car escort to protect the public from Dave's tattoo.

When I got up the next morning, I figured there would be hell to pay at the breakfast table. Jeri and Ollie were still asleep, but Mom and Dad were already up, and Mom had made waffles. More than that, they smiled at me as I sat down. I glanced warily from one to the other. They both looked as though they hadn't slept the rest of the night. I was sorry that Dave's dumb joke had involved them.

They were sorry, too.

"George, we just feel so bad about Dave Hahn," Mom said.

I stopped chewing suddenly and stared at her. I was afraid maybe he'd jumped out a window or something and made the morning paper. "What happened?" I asked.

She and Dad looked at me strangely.

"We're sorry about last *night*," Mom said. "His carrying on that way in public. But what can you *expect*, his father being what he is."

It takes Dad, sometimes, to translate for her.

"It's clear where Dave is headed, that's what she means," he said. "But there's no reason you can't go on being friends, within limits."

I started chewing again and took a sip of milk. They thought Dave Hahn was gay—just because his dad was bisexual and Dave had mooned an elderly couple in a blue Pontiac who must have flagged down the first policeman to go by. I wanted to tell them that Dave has slept with three girls that I knew of, and probably a lot more. I wanted to tell them that he's known all over school as a stud. But I couldn't. I went on chewing.

Dad smiled at me across the table. It was a tight smile, as though there were wires attached to his cheeks. "I know you're as ashamed of what happened last night as we are, George, but that's all behind us now. It's time to turn over a new leaf. I'm taking next week off and we're going to fly out east—just the two of us—and see some colleges, look some places over, have ourselves a time. What do you say to that?"

FOUR

Thirty thousand feet above Lake Ontario, the stewardess gave us lunch—some kind of cold meat with a green sauce on top, and chocolate pudding. While Dad was talking to her, I slipped him all my green sauce. After I tasted the pudding, I slipped him that, too.

"College-hunting, I'll bet," the stewardess said, pouring more coffee for Dad.

He beamed. He gets this certain smile on his face when he talks to a pretty woman. Even his voice sounds different. More gentle. Chivalrous.

"I'm taking him back to my old Alma Mater," he said, hoping, I'll bet, she'd ask which one. Then, before she could get away, he told her. "Harvard," he said.

This time the stewardess smiled down at me.

"Good luck," she said, and I couldn't tell if her eyes were laughing or not.

Dad had said that we could visit three schools, and since he was paying for the trip, he ought to be able to choose two of the three—Harvard and Yale, of course—but that I could choose the third.

"University of Miami," I'd said, without even thinking.

I could tell by the look on Dad's face that the offer didn't extend to Florida.

"Northeastern United States, preferably," Dad said. "What about Brown, Columbia, Cornell, Dartmouth . . . ?"

"Swarthmore," I said. It was the first school that came to mind. I didn't even know where it was.

"Good college" said Dad, but he wasn't exactly turning handsprings. "It's Quaker, though, you know."

"I want to visit Swarthmore," I repeated. Maybe all the professors looked like the man on the oatmeal box, but I had to save face.

"Okay," said Dad. "Pennsylvania we can manage."

We'd started out the trip all right. I'd brought along a deck of cards, and Dad and I played a couple hands of Crazy Eights. You can't sit very long on a plane, though, without someone putting food in front of you, so while Dad ate the meat with the green stuff on top, I thumbed through *The Insider's Guide to Colleges* that I'd picked up at a bookstore before we left. *Written by students, for students—what the colleges are really like*, it said on the cover.

I suppose the guidebook said some good things about Harvard, but that wasn't what I was looking for. I ran my finger down the first paragraph:

> . . . *The Harvard insignia is associated with power, prestige, and wealth. . . . This leads us to the obvious conclusion that Harvard is an elitist university for the elite. . . .*

Then I found a paragraph on the next page that really cracked me up. "Hey, Dad," I said, nudging him, "read this."

> ... But the feeling that there are basically three types of students on campus (wonks, jocks, and preppies) seems to be as accurate as ever. Wonks are the nerds who, given a choice between a night in the library and a pair of tickets to the World Series, select the former. Jocks are those who would give up eleven term credits for tickets to a game in the American Soccer League (with a few beers thrown in). Preppies are just that, the Exeter and St. Paul graduates who walk around in Brooks Brothers cords and L.L. Bean hunting boots.
>
> The problem with all students here is that they are taught to think, talk, and act in a certain way: obnoxious, superior, and self-confident. So they do. ...

I don't know why I thought Dad would laugh. "Whoever wrote that is an ass," he said. "I went through Harvard Law School and never saw a wonk in my life."

After an hour or so, I reached down to put the *Insider's Guide* in my gym bag under the seat, and noticed an envelope that Mom must have stuck in.

To read on the plane, she had written on the front. I opened the envelope and pulled out a quiz she had clipped from a magazine.

You'd think that Mom, being a teacher, would

be sick of tests. She's not. She loves them. She takes every quiz in sight, putting her answers on a separate sheet of paper so she can pass the tests on to Jeri and me: *The Great American Values Test; Your Leadership Potential; Your Hostility Profile; Are You a Romantic?* . . . The do-it-yourself test Mom had chosen for me to take on the trip was called *Your Introvert-Extrovert Ratio: How It Can Affect Your Career.*

While Dad was settling back with a crossword puzzle, I looked the quiz over:

For every one of the questions below, circle the response that most often applies to you:

1. *When entering a roomful of strangers, I:*
   A. *Single out one person and start a conversation*
   B. *Smile and wait until I am approached*
   C. *Head for the bar*
   D. *Find an excuse to leave*

2. *My idea of an enjoyable evening is:*
   A. *A large party with many new faces*
   B. *A small dinner with friends*
   C. *An intimate evening with one person*
   D. *A few hours alone doing the things I love*

3. *When called upon to speak in public.* . . .

I crammed the test into the ashtray of my armrest and turned my attention to the window. I was remembering back to ninth grade, when I had to give a talk in Oral Communication—some dumb thing like "How to Trace Your Family Tree." The evening before the talk, I had a panic attack. I told Dad I didn't think I could do it.

"Look at it this way," Dad had said. "If you were going to address the Minnesota Bar Review, you just might have reason to shake a little. But of all the speeches being given in the city tomorrow, yours is probably the least important. Of all the speeches being given in the state of Minnesota, yours is the least significant. Of all the speeches being given in the United States, yours hardly amounts to a gurgle. . . ."

By the time Dad got to the United Nations, my speech was merely a speck of dust in the cosmos, so I'd told him it obviously didn't make any difference whether I gave it or not.

I gave the speech.

The pilot's voice came over the intercom and said we would be landing at Boston's Logan Airport in ten minutes. The stewardess came by to collect our trays, Dad straightened his tie, and I clutched the armrests as we made our descent and prepared for my interview at Harvard.

By six that evening, we were sitting in a seat on Amtrak, heading for New Haven. Dad and I were barely speaking.

"You walked in there with a chip on your shoulder," he said at last.

I'd been reading more of *The Insider's Guide,* mostly to keep from talking to Dad. *One crucial point,* it said, *keep your parents at least a thousand feet and preferably a thousand miles away from the interview session. . . .*

"How do you know?" I asked him.

"I was watching from down the hall. You walked in with your shoulders slumped and that hangdog look on your face. Might as well have worn a sign saying 'kick me.' "

"They weren't exactly friendly," I answered.

"It's all an *act!*" Dad said earnestly. "They just want to see how you respond."

"Could have fooled me," I told him.

Dad opened the pages of his *Wall Street Journal*, then closed them again. "Did you tell them that I'm an alumnus?"

"*You* told them that, Dad. How else do you think I got the interview? The man said he hardly ever conducts an interview before he's seen the application."

"So whose fault is that?" Dad countered. "We've been after you for weeks to get those applications in the mail."

"Look!" I said. "It was your idea to fly out here, not mine. I'm not *ready* for an interview. I've got a lot more thinking to do."

"So do your thinking later!" Dad said in exasperation. I could tell he was getting really sick of me. "Nobody's asking you to decide anything right this minute. All you have to do is apply, get the ball rolling." He opened the *Wall Street Journal* again, giving the pages a hard shake, cracking them into position. "Life's going to pass you by, George. Opportunity's going to take one look at you and go the other way."

We fell into silence again. I tried to picture it, me sitting in the grass somewhere and this big yellow box labeled "opportunity" stopping to look me over. I must have been smiling because Dad cracked his newspaper again, even louder, and I wiped the smile off my face, folded my hands over my stomach, and watched the lights whiz by in the growing darkness beyond the window.

The interview at Harvard hadn't gone well at all. It was one of those situations where the harder you try not to say something stupid, the more stupid it sounds when you say it. There was one awful moment, after I'd been asked how I spent last summer and what books I'd read lately, when the man just grew silent. Just sat there looking at me, and I was staring down at this thread on the sleeve of my jacket, wondering whether or not to pull it. I realized I was sitting with one foot resting on top of the other, too, like a country hick, but I knew if I moved it then he'd be sure to notice. I thought of a dozen things to say to break the silence, but they all seemed too stupid for words.

I had just taken hold of the thread and was ready to give it a yank when the man said, "What do you consider your worst faults?"

Oh, God, I'd thought. *Sitting there like a brick was one. Wearing a blue blazer with threads at the seam was another. The Insider's Guide* said that the most important thing about the interview was to give the other guy a good time. *If you can make the interviewer laugh or interest him with your unorthodox or forthright views,* it said, *you have a good chance of success.*

When he asked my worst faults, I could have looked at my watch and quipped, "How much time do you have?" and made him laugh.

I could have said, "This week or last?"

Instead, I pulled hard at the thread on my jacket, puckering the cloth along the seam, and said, "I

38

guess I'd have to think about that one awhile." Like I'm so perfect or something.

The interview was over after that. The guy shook my hand and said he was glad to meet me and how I should remember there were a whole lot of good schools out there besides Harvard and that it wouldn't be the end of the world if I didn't get in.

I already knew that I didn't belong. It was like all the people I saw had these big brains pressing against the insides of their skulls. The professors all looked busy and brilliant, hurrying off to some international conference or something, and I just knew if I said "hello," they'd answer me in Latin.

I didn't go for an interview at Yale. In New Haven the next morning, Dad and I just walked around looking at the Gothic buildings with their turrets and spires, and the huge iron gates of the courtyards that probably clanked shut each night, like a prison. CLASS OF 1773, it read on a statue of Nathan Hale, and engraved around the top of the pedestal were the words, "I only regret that I have but one life to lose for my country." I stood there looking at Nathan, with his wrinkled shirt and scuffed shoes. Put him in Levi's and he bore an uncanny resemblance to me. I wondered if Dad noticed.

"Fine young man," Dad murmured beside me.

I swallowed as we started off again. Part of me was furious at Dad for arranging this stupid trip. Another part was grateful that he cared. Despite the fiasco at Harvard, he was making a super effort to get along. He'd wanted this to be a good time for us both—two old buddies going off to look over the old colleges; wanted to get back some of the camaraderie we used to have. I knew it for sure when, in a coffee shop near campus that noon, Dad said, "Now there's a foxy chick."

I swallowed a bite of hamburger and hoped nobody heard. I hadn't heard anybody call a girl a "foxy chick" since fourth grade. Slowly I turned and looked where Dad was looking. A dark-haired girl sat at a table by the window pulling the toothpicks out of her club sandwich. She had on three different shirts, each one larger than the next, in shades of orange and yellow. There was a purplish scarf draped loosely around her neck, the kind of casual toss that somehow you know she spent ten minutes in front of the mirror getting right. She had a sort of ethereal look about her that told me she was reading a collection of French sonnets. I didn't belong at Yale either. That wasn't my life, it was Dad's. *I only regret that I have but one life to live for my father.* As soon as I'd finished my hamburger, I said, like a sullen ingrate, "Can we go? Are we through?"

We headed for the airport for a plane to Philadelphia, where we'd rent a car and drive to Swarthmore.

"You know," Dad said as we waited in line at the ticket counter, "it wouldn't hurt to see Princeton while we're here in the East. Wouldn't be much out of the way at all."

Something seemed to grow heavier inside my chest, pressing against my ribs. I could feel the throb of pulse in my temples.

"I don't want to see Princeton," I said darkly. "I don't even want to see Swarthmore. I didn't want to come in the first place. It was all your idea."

I never saw Dad look at me the way he did then. It was a hurt, questioning look, and I was on the verge of apologizing when it was our turn at the counter. Dad's face suddenly frosted over.

"Two tickets to Minneapolis," he said. "How do we get there from here?"

I don't think we said anything at all on the way home. Dad worked on some papers he'd brought along in a briefcase, and I sat beside him pretending to sleep, but it was only because I didn't have anything to read. *The Insider's Guide* had already caused enough trouble. I would even have taken the quiz Mom sent, just for something to do, if I'd still had it.

I knew I had been ungrateful. Dad had taken three days off work, which was a sacrifice you wouldn't believe. I felt miserable, but something told me that if I didn't stand up to him now, I'd be lost. If I let him put me on the old railroad, I'd never get off, and before you knew it, Jeri and Ollie would be on it, too. Somebody had to look out for them. Especially for Ollie.

I guess I worry about Ollie more than anyone else in our family. Jeri's smart—brain-smart, I mean—but Ollie's different. I don't think you could call him dumb, exactly—just slow. Once he catches onto something, he's got it and doesn't forget, but it takes him a while to understand.

Mom says it's his attention span. She says he lets his eyes wander when he's supposed to be reading, and if he looks up every time someone enters the room, it's bound to take him all night to read a chapter. Dad says Ollie just doesn't "apply himself." I don't know. I've watched the kid study—the way he frowns down at the book, twists a lock of hair around and around his finger, squirms, sighs. . . . He tries. He really does. But "slow" isn't a word that Mom and Dad can accept.

Dad reached up and adjusted the light above his seat, then went on working. He was holding a contract of some kind, in small print, the sort of thing that would take me a couple of hours to read. But Dad just breezed along, making checks in the margin here and there with a red pen.

I suppose the two smartest people in our family are Dad and Trish. Patricia, in fact, is about Most Perfect Everything: Most Perfect Daughter, Most Perfect Student, Most Perfect Teenager, Most Perfect Bride. . . . Especially Most Perfect Bride.

The wedding had Mom mesmerized for five months. It was scheduled for May, but the moment the engagement announcement appeared in the *Minneapolis Tribune,* the preparations went into high gear. Every few weeks Trish had to fly back from New York for another fitting or something, and Mom even commissioned Aunt Sylvia to make a needlepoint pillow for the ring-bearer. It had a satin ruffle around the edge and two satin ribbons sewn on top to tie the ring on so it wouldn't fall off. But get this: the ring was fake. The best man would keep the real ring in his pocket. Seven weeks of needlepoint just so some four-year-old cousin could walk down the aisle holding a pillow with a fake ring.

Meanwhile, Trish was trying to finish her second year of college, and we found out she'd been battling an ulcer all semester. The day after finals, she flew home, saw the doctor, got a prescription, and the following day she was married.

The stewardess came by and asked Dad if he'd like a drink.

"No, thanks," he said, and went on working. Any other time he would have turned to me and said, "How about you, George? Want a Coke or something?" This time it was like I wasn't even there. The stewardess looked at me, and I just shook my head. The plane droned on, heading back to Minnesota in the dark.

I was thinking about the champagne we drank at Trish's wedding.

"You ought to offer a toast to your sister," Dad had told me behind the stephanotis, just after he'd said how happy he was and how he wished she had waited till she'd graduated, both in the same breath. So after everyone sat down at the tables with the cream-colored roses in the center, I stood up to make a toast, but nobody noticed. I picked up my butter knife and hit it against the side of my water glass a couple times. The room grew still.

"To the happy couple," I'd said, raising my champagne glass. "I . . . uh . . . guess the traditional thing to say is that I'm not losing a sister, I'm gaining a brother-in-law." The guests laughed politely, but I felt something cold on my shoe. I moved my foot. "Well," I said, "I've known Trish ever since she was a little girl . . ." More laughter. ". . . and I want to say that Roger couldn't be marrying a nicer person." Something cold was running down my pant leg. I looked. There was a puddle of water on the table, trickling over the edge in a steady stream. I realized I had cracked my glass with the butter knife. "To Trish and Roger," I said. "Here's wishing them the best of luck." I sat down before I realized there was water on my chair as well.

A week after the wedding, Ollie and I had sat

out on the porch eating lunch and looking at Trish's wedding picture in the paper. Ollie had leaned on my shoulder, his jaws moving against my shirt as he chewed his sandwich. I was reading about how the bride's father was senior partner in the law firm of Richards, Barnes, and Marks. "She is the granddaughter of Horace L. Richards, founder of the firm," the paper said, "and grandniece of the late Elberta Hampton, on her mother's side, who was, for seven years, the president of the Women's Historical Society of Greater Minneapolis."

The writeup had said that Trish was a student at Cornell University where her husband had graduated *summa cum laude*.

"What's that mean?" Ollie had asked, pointing to the words and leaving a trace of peanut butter on the page, for which Mom would kill him.

"It's Latin," I'd said. "With highest honors."

Ollie continued to point to the Latin words, one at a time. "With," he repeated, pointing to *summa*, "highest," pointing to *cum*, "honors," pointing to *laude*.

"No, actually it reads, 'highest with praise,' " I'd told him, "but we just call it, 'with highest honors.' "

Ollie had looked at me blankly, then wiped his hand across his mouth. "That's why I get mixed up," he said. "Words never say what they mean, do they, George?"

Dad put his papers away finally, closed his briefcase, and leaned back against the seat. I couldn't tell if his eyes were closed or not. He was very quiet, and I knew what he was thinking.

I don't care, I told myself. *I'm doing it for Ollie.*

FIVE

Things were pretty stiff around our house that fall. Dad and I spoke to each other—"Pass the mustard," "Lock the door," "Where's the sports page?"—stuff like that, but you wouldn't call us close, exactly. I think both of us felt bad about it, but at the same time, each of us felt that he was right. And when Ollie brought home his first report card from seventh grade, all C's except for a D in Spanish, I overheard Dad say to Mom in the kitchen, "Well, I wonder what the *next* disappointment will be?"

There's something about knowing you're a disappointment to your parents that's hard to take. Parents think we don't care, but we do. I know that Ollie cared. It seemed to me that Ollie had spent half his life trying to please them, but he never seemed to measure up.

I used to think about that a lot—measuring up. Think about whose yardstick it was, anyway, and how do parents know that, with all our faults, we just might not grow up to be famous or something? I mean, if anybody had expected Henry Ford or Thomas Edison to be great when they were grown, do you suppose they would ever have been yelled at? If anyone knew what Abraham Lincoln would become, don't you think people would have treated him with more respect when he was little?

I tried this out on Dad, though, when I was Ollie's age. He'd been putting up storm windows, and all afternoon he'd had me bringing him things like I was a slave or something—a screwdriver, a rag, a bucket, a hammer. . . . When I sprawled out on the couch at last and Dad finally sat down to read the paper, I said, "Listen, Dad, I just want you to know that the kid you kick around may design your car someday; the boy you boss might just publish your newspaper."

Dad lowered his head and stared at me over his glasses. "And just remember," he'd said, "that if it wasn't for *me*, you wouldn't be sitting there at all with one hand in the potato chips and your feet on the coffee table."

It had become a family joke, and we'd all laughed about it afterward, but now, out in the kitchen, no one was laughing. In fact, I could tell from snatches of conversation that the talk had turned from Ollie to me, and how I'd botched my interview at Harvard.

"Just goes through life like he hasn't a worry in the world," Dad was saying.

I could hardly believe he'd said that. Me? Not a worry in the world? Maybe I didn't worry about the same things Dad did, but the first memory I had was of me worrying. Standing in nursery school wondering whether Mom would pick me up. When I was a little kid, in fact, somebody should have told me about crime and war and pollution, because I worried about all the wrong things. While adults were worrying about the Mideast crisis, I was worrying about how I'd find my way home again when I got my first job.

It was kindergarten when I started worrying about marriage. There were only two girls who spoke to me at all; one with a tooth missing and another who made noises at me behind the paint easel. I panicked. I was afraid that by the time I grew up, the prettiest girls would be taken. I asked my teacher if she'd marry me, and she said yes, if I still wanted her when I was twenty. For a whole month I was in Nirvana. Five years old, and I'd already proposed and been accepted.

Dad must not have known me well when I was seven, either. Seven's the worst. I wouldn't be seven again for a million dollars. I'd had so many compulsions it's a wonder I could function at all. Like eating everything on my plate counterclockwise and reversing the direction for dessert; like scratching my head and sniffing my fingers; like licking the rear window of the car. But now here were Mom and Dad in the kitchen, talking about Ollie's grades and how I let opportunity pass me by and how Trish, who was seeing a doctor for stomach problems, should have waited until after she'd graduated to marry.

"You're next on the agenda," I said to Jeri as I passed her going out, but she didn't know what I was talking about. And maybe she wasn't on the agenda. Jeri's grades were straight A's, except for B's in Phys Ed. Jeri glided through school hardly opening a book, while Ollie agonized over page after page.

There was something about Dad's comment that stuck with me the rest of the evening—the wondering what the next disappointment would be. It was his own disappointment he was talking about, not mine or Ollie's, as though what we were feeling didn't matter.

Bud Irving turned eighteen in November, and we celebrated by going to the 18-20 Club. Most of the time it's a singles bar, but on the second Friday of every month, they don't let you in unless you're between eighteen and twenty. So Bud went in first, showed his ID, then snuck around to the side door and opened it for Dave Hahn, Psycho, and me.

"What's that?" I asked Bud, looking at the big tag he was wearing with his initials on it.

"You've got to wear it if you want to play Selectrocution," he said. It was the game we'd all heard about.

"What if somebody else already has your initials?" I asked him.

"You use another combination," he said. I should have been able to figure that out for myself. People were walking by with initials reading "EZ," "PM," "XS," "OO," and "QT."

At the bar, they only sold near-beer, soft drinks, and coffee. Discount brought a bunch of Cokes over to our table near the dance floor, and we sat there drinking, trying to figure out the system.

Bud was explaining the ballot they gave him at the door.

"You put your initials at the top, like this," he said, "and here, underneath, you're supposed to put the initials of the five girls you find most attractive."

"LT," Psycho said right off as a red-haired girl walked by.

"NS," I said to Bud, watching a pretty girl on the dance floor.

"Around midnight," Bud went on, teaching his little flock, "the ballots are collected, the computer goes to work, and the person who was voted for the most number of times wins the contest."

"And. . . ?" I said.

"You get your ballot back with stars beside the initials of the girls who voted for you in return. If *nobody* voted for you, your card says, 'sorry, you have just been selectrocuted.' "

"You're kidding!" said Dave.

"No, I'm not! Some people actually go outside and get sick," Bud told us. There was something enormously comforting about not having to wear the initials and play the game. While Bud kept pushing back his hair and looking about nervously, the rest of us sat there smirking, nudging him when we saw a good-looking girl go by.

All the while the eyeballing went on, people were sending messages to each other on a video screen. Anyone, Bud said, could send a message. All you had to do was write it on one of the index cards provided and give it to the man who was typing the letters. We'd look up at the screen above the bar and read, *H.N. Female: You're hotter than hot. I'd do anything to dance with you. P.L.* or *D.A. Male: Tickle me with your mustache. Girl in polka dots.* You could even sign your name "Anonymous" if you wanted.

The room was smoky. A thick gray haze floated by the red and blue lights near the ceiling. All around the room, people were on the move, initials in search of initials.

"A real meat market," Dave said. We watched the dancers.

Suddenly Psycho gave me a nudge. "You're on," he said. I didn't know what he meant. Then I saw a message moving across the screen. *To male in red polo:* it said. *Make my day. Ask me to dance. CC.* Each message was repeated twice.

"Jeez!" I said. I wasn't wearing a tag! I'd thought I was safe! I tried to look around without moving my head. "What do I do, Discount?"

"Try to find her," he said. "She's probably watching you right now."

I turned to the left and there she was at a table against the wall with two other girls. They were all looking our way and smiling. CC was plump and pretty.

I stood up.

"What the heck," said Discount, following me over to the girls' table. Dave came, too, and we each asked a girl to dance. Psycho stayed where he was, looking relieved.

I moved self-consciously around the floor with CC. She beamed and didn't take her eyes off me. The music, unfortunately, was slow, so we held hands and danced.

"Come here often?" I asked her. Mr. Original himself.

"Second Friday of every month," she said, still beaming. "How about you?"

"My first time," I answered.

"Like it?"

"I just got here," I told her.

"Lucky me," she said.

It wasn't that she was plump that turned me off, it was the way she kept grinning at me, like now that she had made the first move, what was I going to do about it? She was probably nineteen. Twenty, even. The music seemed to go on forever. The room was getting more noisy, and when CC said something else, I had to ask her to repeat it. She was talking about a party later. I told her I'd hurt my ankle and couldn't go, which was about the dumbest thing in the world, because there I was dancing on it. When the music stopped, CC just turned her back on me and lit a cigarette.

"I bombed," I said, back at the table.

"I think her friend's twenty-one," Dave told me. "She had me pegged, all right. Asked if I was still in high school."

We sat there comparing notes and nursing our egos. An hour into the evening, though, our skins were a little tougher and we were sending messages with the best of them. I sent all of mine anonymous. At first I was picking all the pretty girls. *Hey, M.D. Female: If you're a doctor, you can operate on me anytime. Anonymous. To E.B. Female: I want to make the blood rush to your head. Anonymous. T.L. Female: I think I love you. Anonymous.* You could say things on that video screen you'd never dare say in person. After a while, though, I got to thinking about all the girls like CC. I leaned my arms on the table and peered through the smog, and every time I saw a girl who didn't quite measure up physically, I sent her a message. *To G.B. Female: Love your hair. Anonymous. K.S. Female: Great legs. Anonymous. To L.L. Female: You make my heart race. Anonymous.* Then I'd watch their eyes light up when a message flashed on the screen. When it came time to vote, I persuaded Bud to write down all their initials on his ballot. Just so they wouldn't get selectrocuted. So they could always wonder who the guy was who thought they were special.

Maybe all the smoke was beginning to affect my brain, because right after I told a tall skinny girl that she must be the majestic queen of a long lost tribe in a previous life, I picked out a short heavy girl and sent her a message that *Someone in this room loves you madly.* I was going to send a message to a girl in a black skirt when Discount told me she was a waitress.

And then I saw another message on the screen. *To male in red shirt: You bring out the animal in me. Let's mate. M.K.*

"Holy cow!" breathed Psycho, in awe.

I could feel the color rising in my face. "Discount," I said, "I'm getting out of here."

"At least see what she looks like," Bud told me.

I pushed away my Coke, though, and had just started for the men's room when I felt a familiar finger in the small of my back, and then I was looking down at Maureen Kimball, with her glow-in-the-dark initials.

"Joke, joke," she grinned. "Were you looking for me or making your escape?"

"I didn't know you were eighteen," I told her, as the music started up again.

"What?" she shouted.

"Didn't know you were eighteen!"

"Last week," she yelled back.

We tried conversation a few more times, but it was impossible. Maureen laid her head against my chest, and we danced close for a while.

I tried to pretend she was a stranger, that I'd never met her before. Tried to feel some kind of attraction—even let my finger slide up and down her backbone, which made her snuggle even closer. I decided that the next time she turned her face up to mine, I'd lean down and kiss her—just sort of brush her lips—maybe do this three times in a row—see if it would ignite a fire in me. But the next time she looked up, she was smiling again and her face was all screwed up, like one of those dolls with the dried apple heads. The music stopped. I took Maureen over to the bar and bought her coffee, then went back to the guys.

Dave and I had to work the next morning and Psycho was sick with worry that someone would send him a message, so we decided not to wait to see how Bud came out in the polls. He turned in his ballot, and we were just making our way toward the door when I grabbed Bud's sleeve and stopped. There was another girl I knew on the dance floor. It was Jeri.

I realized that I had been watching her dance, knowing she looked familiar somehow in the dimly lit room, but it hadn't registered that she was my sister. For one thing, she was wearing a skirt with slits up the sides, high-heeled shoes, and a sweater that came down snug over her hips. Her hair was different, too. She was slow-dancing with a guy who looked to be twenty, her arms draped about his neck, their noses touching, bodies scarcely moving. He had a marine haircut.

I waited till the music stopped, then went over.

"Oh, God," Jeri breathed when she saw me, and turned away.

The guy looked at me, then at Jeri.

"My brother," she told him.

"Hello," I said, and then, to her, "What are you doing here, Jeri? How'd you get in?"

"I could ask you the same thing," she retorted.

"Who you with?"

"She's with me," said the marine.

Jeri just laughed. "No, I'm not. Some guy from school got me in."

"Mother know you're here?"

"She know *you're* here?" Jeri looked at me defiantly, grabbed the marine's hand, and moved off through the crowd.

I went to Little Mexico later with the guys for a taco salad, then home. The lamp was still on in the upstairs hall. Mom always leaves it on after she goes to bed, and the rule is that the last person home turns it off. Then if she wakes up during the night and sees that the light is out, she'll know everyone's safely in and can go back to sleep. Jeri's bedroom door was still open, so I left the lamp on.

Couldn't sleep, though. Every time a car went by, I'd rise up on one elbow and look out the window. After a while I stopped looking, just listened—listened for the sound of a car stopping, Jeri getting out. It was after two when she finally came home and I heard the door click.

Mom'll kill her, I thought. But Jeri came softly upstairs, turned off the lamp, and went on into her room without making a sound. Mom must have been asleep. I was the one who lay there awake until three.

Trish and Roger didn't make it home for Thanksgiving, but Grandpa Richards came for dinner as well as Dad's sister, Sylvia, and her husband. With all the chairs filled at the table, we didn't miss Trish as much as we might have.

"This means she'll come for Christmas," Mom said, to console herself.

Grandpa Richards is always on the sour side. Even when he smiles, the corners of his mouth turn down just a little. "Prickly," is the way Mom describes him; you have to be careful what you say because you never know when he's going to take offense. Aunt Sylvia couldn't be more different. You never have to wonder what she's thinking, because she tells you, in a way that couldn't possibly offend. Unless, of course, you're Grandpa Richards. Which is probably why her husband rarely says anything at all. Uncle Lawrence just sits around sucking on his pipe, looking amiable and agreeing with everybody in turn, even when they contradict each other. I was glad, actually, when everyone had gone. It wasn't that Thanksgiving was so awful; it was just such an effort.

It was probably because we were still on edge that there was a flareup that evening. As the dining room table was cleared of plates and the dishwasher started its second load, Mom made space for Ollie at one end of the table and sat him down with his Spanish book and the assignment he was supposed to have turned in the day before.

Jeri had done her part with the dishes and gone upstairs, and I was sprawled on the sofa with the comics, waiting for the dishwasher to cut off so I could unload it again. From out in the kitchen, I could hear the clink of Dad's knife against the cutting board as he carved all the meat off the turkey, dividing it into packs for the freezer, which he neatly labeled "Sandwich slices," "Dark meat," and "Giblets." In between the clinks of the knife, I could hear the soft whomp of Typhus's tail on the linoleum, waiting for a piece of turkey to fall off the table.

I had just finished Doonesbury and Spiderman and was turning to Apartment 3-G when I happened to glance at Ollie in the next room. There was something about the way he was sitting, dwarfed by the china cupboard behind him and the grandfather clock in one corner, his head tipped forward, chin resting against his chest, that made me think he was crying. Just the way he kept one hand over his eyes, maybe. And then, as I watched, I saw his shoulders rise, grow rigid, then sink again, saw his chin drop even lower and his lips open. He was crying silently, scribbling all the while with his pencil.

Something ballooned inside my chest—a kind of sadness that was almost pain. I fastened my eyes on Spiderman, but they kept traveling back to the dining room, and the way Ollie was bravely keeping his tears to himself. If I'd taken Spanish instead of French, I could have gone out and helped him. I was trying to decide what to do when Mom came in from the kitchen with the meat platter and put it in the china cupboard. She glanced at Ollie's book as she passed.

"You're still on the same page you were twenty minutes ago," she said, not even looking at him. "Well, if you want to spend your whole weekend on this assignment, that's all right with me."

I saw Ollie's shoulders heave once more, saw one hand furtively wipe the tears off his cheek.

He leaned closer to the paper and scribbled even harder. Mom went back out to the kitchen.

The next time she came in, however, carrying the gravy bowl, Ollie said, in his usual soft voice, "I think I'm going to drop Spanish next semester."

"Don't be ridiculous," Mom said. She opened the china cupboard again and put the bowl inside.

"It's too *hard!*" Ollie said, a little louder, and I wondered if I was the only one who caught the quaver in his voice. I wasn't. Typhus wandered in from the kitchen and came over to stand by Ollie, her nose on Ollie's thigh. Then she plopped down on the rug beside him, watching with mournful eyes.

Mom turned and addressed Ollie's back. This time her voice was a bit softer, but she still didn't seem to know he'd been crying. "You can't go through life dropping out when things get difficult," she told him. "That's what you said about clarinet lessons, Ollie. That's what you said about the science fair and the merit badge in astronomy."

I thought about that a moment. Those were all things that Mom and Dad had chosen, not Ollie. Ollie had wanted to join the Scouts because he loved camping out. Two weeks after he'd signed up, Dad started him working on a merit badge— had his Scouting career all laid out before him: Tenderfoot as soon as he could make it, Second Class by age thirteen, First Class by fourteen, then Star, Life, and Eagle. You couldn't just be a Scout in our family; you had to be the best there was.

"Maybe Spanish *is* too hard for him, Mom," I said from the couch.

Mom's eyes met mine in a direct line: "Well, hard or not, he can't get into college without it."

"But maybe he's not cut out for college," I ventured, getting bolder.

There were footsteps in the kitchen and Dad came to the doorway, sleeves rolled up, tie loose. He and Mom were both looking at me now, and even Ollie lifted his eyes and peered at me over one arm.

"What I mean is," I said, "has anyone asked *him* what he wants to do?"

"I certainly don't recall asking *your* opinion," Dad challenged.

I'd started it, though, and I wasn't about to give up. "Even if he does decide on college, he doesn't have to take a foreign language till he gets to high school," I argued. "He's got a few more years to decide. Spanish might be easier for him then."

"And it just might be more difficult if he doesn't get a head start now," Mother said.

"Don't give advice about Ollie's life until you've got your own in order," Dad told me. He turned to Ollie again, and this time his voice was more gentle: "Problem with you is, you don't try, Ollie. You think that if you put something off long enough, you can get out of it."

"I do *not!*" Ollie said hotly. "I *try,* Dad, but I can't spend my whole *life* studying! I've got other things to do, too."

That really triggered something in Dad. "There are *always* other things! That's the trouble! That's it right there! Well, let me tell you something, young man: You're not going to do another thing this weekend, not going to go anywhere, until all your homework's done—math, Spanish, English, whatever."

"Dad, there's a campout tomorrow!" Ollie protested.

"You can forget the campout."

Ollie dropped his pencil and this time his chin quivered noticeably. "I'll finish Spanish before I go, but I can do the rest when I get back."

"I said *now!*" Dad roared. "You're not leaving this house until every single assignment is done."

Ollie's head bent down again and I saw the way his mouth opened, saw the shake of his shoulders, and suddenly I threw down the comics. With Mom and Dad watching, I stormed across the living room, up the stairs, and banged my door as hard as I could. The walls shook; the windows rattled. Any minute I expected Dad to come up and whack me on the side of the head, but he just yelled up the stairs after me instead.

I stood in the middle of the floor, fists clenched, feeling the blood throb in my temples. I was surprised to discover that there were tears in my own eyes—tears for Ollie, not for me.

Two hours later, I came downstairs with the stack of college applications all filled out, sealed, and neatly stamped. I put them by the door as I got my jacket.

"Well," Dad said, looking over. "Now that's more like it. Something *constructive*, for a change."

I didn't answer. I got my keys, drove to the post office, and mailed the applications for the pickup next morning.

SIX

Trish came home for Christmas bringing Roger and a bottle of Maalox with her. Since Mom and Dad didn't want her to quit college while Roger was in graduate school, and Trish didn't want them supporting her and Roger, she compromised by signing up for nine credits at Cornell, working in a department store in the afternoons, and taking a tablespoon of Maalox after every meal.

"Tell me why she's so stubborn!" Dad said at dinner one night while Trish and her husband were out. "She's never been like this before. If she's touchy about money, she could pay it back eventually—consider it a loan. There's absolutely no reason for her to work."

"When I think of all that talent going to waste. . . !" said Mom. "The girl gets a scholarship in art, and she's selling draperies!"

"Maybe she just wants to run her own life," I put in. But I could tell it wasn't appreciated, so I didn't say any more.

Jeri and Ollie said nothing. Ollie just stared down at his plate while he mauled his lima beans. I'd swear he was eating everything counterclockwise the way I used to do, studying each bite before he put it in his mouth. Jeri, on the other hand, was just marking time. Even when she wasn't wearing headphones, she drummed her fingers on the table and nodded her head to some inner beat, ignoring the gale warnings around her, escaping as soon as she could to her room.

Christmas went all right, actually. It's sort of understood in our family that quarrels are put on the shelf for the holidays. We make a tremendous effort to get along, and there were times I caught Mom and Dad looking at us—at me, in particular —with a sort of wistful, puzzled look, wishing, I suppose, that we could use this truce to sort things out. It bothered me more than I let on.

What *was* the problem in our family, exactly? Dad and Mom must have loved us or they probably wouldn't have wanted us in the first place. I can't believe they wanted us to be unhappy, either. *What,* then?

They wanted us to be something we weren't, something that would make them really proud of us. Success by their own definition. I mean, wonderful, successful children must have come from wonderful, successful parents. Isn't that what it's all about? It had been done to them by their own parents, I guess, and to the parents by the grandparents, and on and on. Where did it start? I didn't know. It was where it was going to end that concerned me.

Even Grandpa Richards seemed reflective. The day after Christmas, I found him stirring the ashes in the fireplace, searching for live coals before he closed the damper. I got the tongs and helped turn over the large log at the back. As

Grandpa poked at it, he said, as if to himself, ". . . and girls all must, As chimney sweepers come to dust."

I didn't know the poem, but it was clear it had something to do with death. I tried to get his mind off what was ahead and focus on all he'd accomplished so far.

"Must feel pretty good, Gramps, to see your granddaughter married now," I said. "She and Roger starting a life together." And when he didn't answer, I added, "Must feel good, too, to have a law firm named after you. I'll be lucky to have a nameplate on a desk somewhere."

Grandpa just grumbled and put the poker back on the stand. I figured he'd make some curt reply, and was surprised when he said, "Well, some of us do the right thing for the wrong reason, and some of us do the wrong thing, but for the right reason."

It sounded so strange coming from Grandpa Richards that I just stood and looked at him. "What do you mean?" I asked finally.

His old crochety self got control once more. "Think it out for yourself, George," he said, and closed the damper with a clank. "Don't always be asking people to explain. Figure it out for yourself."

I retreated back into my shell after New Year's. Ollie had barely passed Introductory Spanish I, and night after night, he sat at the dining room table, books spread out around him, laboriously memorizing verb tenses for Introductory Spanish II. Mom would call Trish every Saturday and ask about her ulcer. Jeri lived in her room, coming out only for meals, and I concentrated on weight-lifting at Psycho's. When the temperature climbed above zero, I'd do some cross-country skiing with Discount, taking Typhus along, maybe—watch the way she leapt in and out of snowdrifts like a ginger-colored porpoise. But most of the time I stayed in. I'd take out my saxophone, maybe, and sit up in my room, playing. Or go over to Bud's and form a combo. Minnesotans are pretty good at doing things indoors. Uptown, in fact, you can go from store to store without stepping outdoors at all, because the buildings are connected with skyways.

The second week of February, I slid in my chair at breakfast and reached for the Rice Chex at the same time Jeri took hold of the box, but this time she let me have it without a fight. She was reading a bright red supplement that had come with the paper, and her hand dropped down onto the table as she slowly turned the pages.

"I don't *believe* this!" she said.

"What?" I asked, pouring milk over the chunks in my bowl and dusting it all with sugar.

"Valentines! Listen:

> *Linda, darling: Understanding*
> *and trust, they are a must. Our*
> *love has grown to heights I'd*
> *never known. Always remember*
> *the love we share, nothing else*
> *can compare. I love you. Ron.*

Mom, *who* would put this stuff in the news-paper?"

"About twenty-five thousand people in Minneapolis and St. Paul," Mom said, standing over by the refrigerator where she was packing a lunch for herself. "The paper said that this was the largest Valentine supplement they'd ever put out."

"You've got to look through all twenty-five thousand to see if you got a Valentine?" I asked, disbelieving.

"They're alphabetical," Jeri said, thrusting the paper at me and reaching for the comics instead. "What nerds!"

LOVE MESSAGES FROM ROMANTICS, it said on the front. I skimmed the pages. The ads went from three lines with no hearts at all to four-inch ads with three hearts at the top and bottom.

Angel. You drive me plum out of my peach orchard. Kevin.

Mrs. Wilson, my love. When you read this, I'll be with you, my sweet dove. You are the wife for the rest of my life. Del.

I couldn't stand any more and passed it along to Ollie. I'd just stuffed the last bite of toast in my mouth when he said, "Hey, George! Here's one for you."

My teeth paused in midbite.

"There are a lot of Georges in the world," I said.

"But this one is to George T. Richards." Ollie leaned over the paper as Jeri looked up. " 'George T. Richards,' it says. 'Make my chimes ring. M.K.' "

I swallowed.

"Who's M.K.?" asked Mother, turning around from the counter.

"Maureen Kimball, I'll bet," said Jeri. "Boy, has she got a case on George!"

"Make my *chimes* ring?" Ollie said, still trying to figure it out. Then he got it and giggled.

Mom gave me a wry smile. "Something here I should know?" she asked.

I got up from the table. "M.K. has chimes where her brains should be," I answered.

When I got to school, though, the guys had already heard, mostly because Maureen was going around telling everyone. "Bong, bong!" people said to me in the corridors, laughing.

I avoided Maureen as long as I could—even taking a different route to physics because I usually met her going to orchestra. But before the morning was over, I felt her finger probing my back.

"Hi, lover," she said.

I forced a frown. "Bong, bong," I said dryly.

She grinned. "Just going for laughs. Where's your sense of humor?"

"Laughs is right," I said. "That stuff ought to be in the comics. You read some of those? People actually think it's poetry."

"George, you take life too seriously, you know that?" She wasn't grinning this time, and she looked a lot better. When Maureen didn't scrunch up her face, she came close to being pretty. "For once in your life," she was saying, "I'd like to see you do something spontaneous and fun."

"Such as . . . ?"

"That's for you to figure out," she said, and walked on without bothering to look back.

"She's asking for it, you know," Dave Hahn told me at lunch. "Some girls get like that. They need it so bad they practically beg."

"She's just kidding," I said.

"You don't get there, somebody else will."

I pretended I didn't hear that.

By the following day, Maureen's dumb valentine had been forgotten, and the big news around school was that Karen Gunderson was wearing the ring that Bob Ellis had given her on Valentine's Day. She just appeared in class with it on her finger—a small, oval diamond—and by the end of second period, the whole school knew that Karen and Bob were engaged: the first couple in our class. The wedding, Karen told someone, was scheduled for summer.

"Man, it makes me feel old!" Discount said as we walked home after school, the snow compact and settled underfoot, gray with exhaust fumes. He was wearing a cap with a flap over the bottom that covered half his face, and his voice came out muffled. My own cheeks felt raw in the cold. "From there it's only a step to babies, mortgages, and mowing the lawn," Discount told me.

"They've been going together a long time," I mused. "Why put it off?"

"Yeah, I guess so. Me, though, I'd take a trip around the world first or something. Live a little."

"I'll take a trip around the world with Karen Gunderson," I said, and we both laughed.

I didn't much care what happened the last half of my senior year. I already had the credits I needed to graduate, so I just coasted. A lot of us did. Our SAT scores, along with last semester's grades, had already been forwarded to the colleges we'd applied to, and unless we really bombed out our last semester, our final grades wouldn't make much difference. It felt sort of useless going to school at all, but I went out of habit, just like I still ate meals with the family out of habit. Table conversations were usually between Mom and Dad or me and Ollie, though we all talked to Typhus when the silence got to be too much. It was as though plexiglass walls had been erected there on the table, dividing us into cubicles. We could see each other, but we didn't communicate. We knew the walls were there, but we weren't sure why or what to do about them.

Mom threw herself into her work, sponsoring her school's science fair, and Dad was representing some big firm uptown that was supposed to have filed a fraudulent tax return. Dinner conversation usually revolved around that.

Sometimes, on weekends, if Ollie wasn't being punished for another assignment he didn't do—*couldn't* do, maybe—I'd take him to a movie or bowling. Try to give the kid some fun. But I could see that, little by little, he was just giving up. He knew that should he, by some miracle, pass Introductory Spanish II, he'd only have Spanish One and Two to take in high school, followed by Spanish Three and Four, algebra, geometry, physics, and calculus. He started blinking his eyes when he talked.

"Ollie, you need a change of contacts or something?" Dad asked him. "What's wrong with your eyes?"

"I don't know," said Ollie.

"Do they hurt? Itch?"

Ollie shook his head.

"Well, try to pay attention to what you're doing. When you feel the need to blink, do something else instead."

"What do you suggest, Dad—a nervous cough?" I threw in, the first time I'd spoken to him in a month.

Dad gave me an icy look, and I returned the stare. It was as cold at our table as it was outside.

"Just hang in there, Ollie," I said later. "Something will happen."

Something did.

Around the middle of March, the seniors started hearing from colleges. Discount got accepted at Carnegie-Mellon, and the guys took a six-pack over to his house to celebrate. The first of our gang to make the break. We gave him the old handshake and the slap on the back and all, but at the same time, Pittsburgh seemed one heck of a ways away.

In the next two weeks, almost all the seniors had heard from at least one of their schools, and every day someone else had an acceptance or rejection to talk about at lunchtime.

Columbia was the first college to write to me. *Dear applicant*, the form letter read, *we regret to inform you* . . . I left the letter on the coffee table where the folks would find it and went up in my room to watch Bill Cosby.

"I know you must be disappointed," Mom said later when I came down for the Keebler chocolate-covered grahams, "but it's only one school. I'm not even sure I'd want you living in New York anyway."

I murmured something and took the cookies up to my room.

Princeton's letter came a day later. *Dear Mr. Richards: After careful consideration, the admissions office is sorry to tell you that* . . .

Mom was indignant. "Well, New Jersey you can do without, too," she said. "You know where I see you, George? In one of those New England colleges, with the fall leaves and the lacrosse games, the skiing. . . . Did you know that tourists have to reserve rooms a *year* in advance if they want to stay in Vermont in the fall?"

"No," I said. "I didn't know that."

Harvard and Yale came exactly on the same day, and I'd swear they were written by the same person: *Dear Prospective Student: It is with real regret that we inform you* . . .

Dad studied the letter from Harvard for a long time. "Well," he said, "it was that interview, no doubt about it. The minute I saw you walk in there with your shoulders slumped . . ." Mom gave him a look, and he stopped.

"You can always go your first two years somewhere else and then transfer," she told me. "Students do that all the time. Once the schools know you're serious, they'll reconsider. Have you heard from Dartmouth yet?"

I shook my head.

Dartmouth came around the first of April, followed by Brown and Cornell a few days later. *Dear Mr. Richards: Dear Sir: Dear Applicant.* . . .

Mother faced me in the living room one afternoon when she got in. She was holding the latest rejection and hadn't even taken her coat off.

"George, I simply can't understand this. Your combined SAT scores were over 1300 and you're twenty-sixth in a class of three hundred fifty."

"I don't know, Mom," I said, and spread the sports section out on my lap.

She stared at me some more. "Most of them didn't even bother to answer personally. You would *think,* after all the work involved in those applications, they could at least call you something besides 'applicant.' "

"Well, some of them did, anyway," I told her.

An acceptance came from the University of Minnesota.

"I didn't even know you'd applied there," said Dad.

"My ace in the hole," I told him.

By April 15, however, the last of the Ivy Leagues had answered, a rejection by the University of Pennsylvania. It was unanimous.

"My gosh!" said Jeri at the dinner table. "If George can't get in any of the Ivy Leagues, how will I?"

"You won't have any trouble," I told her. "Your grades are better than mine."

"Not *that* much better," Jeri commented. Strangely, she and I were talking again.

"You going to college in Minneapolis, George?" Ollie asked hopefully.

"Looks that way," I told him.

Mom and Dad said nothing. The salt and pepper were passed back and forth across the table along with the Worcestershire sauce. Mom hadn't even changed out of her school clothes. Sometimes, when she's really upset, she forgets to change. Dad's face had that wired look again. His lips opened only wide enough to admit his fork, then clamped shut like a Venus fly trap.

I took Ollie with me that evening to weight-lift

at Psycho's. We read in *Muscle Fitness* magazine that weight-lifting doesn't stunt your growth after all, so I was starting Ollie out on a program to build up his biceps and traps where it would be noticed the most. We'd work on the rest later. Psycho gave him an old T-shirt with the words "Live Bait" on the front, and we worked him for an hour or so. Afterward Ollie's legs were wobbly, but he smiled all the way home. Couldn't stop smiling.

When we stepped inside, though, Mom and Dad weren't smiling. They were sitting side by side on the couch with a handful of papers spread out on the coffee table. Jeri was sitting over on the stairs, as though ready to flee the room at any moment. At first I thought Jeri was in some kind of trouble. Then, when I saw the look on Dad's face, I knew it was me. Even now, I don't think I could describe that look—a mixture of disappointment and rage. Disbelief, maybe.

"Sit down," he said.

"What's wrong?"

"I said sit down!" he roared, and I sat. By the time my hands had touched my knees, however, I knew what was the matter.

"You've been in my desk," I said to Mom.

"Yes, I have," Mom said, and her voice shook. "I did something I've never done before, and I know I shouldn't have, but I had to find out."

I didn't answer.

"Find out what?" ventured Ollie.

Mother picked up a sheet of yellow tablet paper with handwriting on one side: " 'How College Life Mirrors the World at Large,' " she read. " 'This question amply illustrates the fact that there are as many boneheads on campus as there are off. The world is full of pretentious people, and the author of this question obviously thought that he could intimidate prospective students by requiring an essay on a subject that is as ridiculous as it is pompous.' " Mother stopped reading and looked straight at me. "Shall I go on?"

I didn't answer. I don't know why I'd kept my scribbled drafts. So I could gloat over them after I'd sent off the typed copies?

She started to read some more, then put that paper down and picked up another: " 'If I could alleviate one of mankind's most pressing problems, I would put men in skirts, because the pressing problem which needs alleviating most is the ironing of men's trousers. . . .' "

"What a jerk!" Jeri murmured from the stairs.

"Did you really think this was amusing?" Mom asked me. "That you could get admitted to a prestigious college by such smart-aleck jokes? That they would admire your cleverness and originality?"

Dad couldn't control himself any longer: "Did you even *think*?" he bellowed, leaning forward, the veins on his neck standing out. I sat stiffly on the chair across from him, my knees trembling with tension, vaguely wondering if this could give him a coronary. Fear alternated with anger inside my chest. Before I could answer, Dad picked up another sheet of tablet paper and began reading: " 'Why did I choose this university? I didn't. My Dad arranged for an interview I didn't want, to a school I never picked, that is full of wealthy snots I couldn't like in a million years.' " Dad's hand was shaking with rage. I'd never seen him so angry. My own anger began to travel up my body like the mercury in a thermometer—past my collar bone and up my throat. "Do you realize how deeply you've embarrassed me?" Dad said.

To tell the truth, I had forgotten exactly what I'd written on the applications, except that for the University of Minnesota, I'd played it straight. It had never occurred to me that Mom would go through my desk—that they would try to figure out *why* no Ivy League school had accepted me. If it had, I would have had my speech all ready. Now, I had to wing it; all I had to go on was feelings.

"*Why*, George?" Mom was saying. "Why did you do it?"

"Because I didn't want to go," I told her. My teeth felt as though they were clamped together, as though my jaws had locked. I actually had trouble talking. Little pains shot up the side of my cheek.

"You got on that plane with me knowing you were going to pull something like this?" Dad asked. "You went through that charade of visiting those schools, secretly sabotaging things at every turn?"

"George, if you didn't want to go, why didn't you just say so?" Mom asked.

"I said it every way I knew how, but you weren't listening," I told her, and now *I* was shouting. My voice didn't sound like mine at all, though— hollow and high, like someone in a tower. Ollie stared at me as if I were somebody else. Jeri, sitting back on the stairs, didn't move a muscle. All eyes were on me. "You don't care about me, you don't care about my education, you only care how it makes *you* look!" I said.

"That was totally uncalled for," said Mother, and there were tears in her eyes.

In order not to see the tears, to not even think about them, I went on yelling: "*Somebody* had to make the break. I'm not going to end up at an Ivy League school with a bottle of Maalox just to please you and Dad."

"George, that's unfair!"

But I was unstoppable now. The words came tumbling out: "Take a good look, Mom. Trish is having stomach problems, Ollie's got a tic. . . ."

"George!"

"Somebody had to break the chain. And you want to know something else? I'm not going to college at all next year. Not even the University of Minnesota."

Dad slowly got to his feet, as though he didn't quite trust himself not to rush me. "Okay, you've said it," he said, and his words seemed like chunks of concrete clunking to the floor. "You're my son, and I'm responsible for your food, shelter, and medical care, but beyond that, you're on your own. You want to live your life without any help from me, you've got it. Anything you want beyond the mere necessities, you buy yourself. Is that understood?"

"Yes," I said, my heart still pounding. "Understood."

"Good," Dad said. He turned and strode out of the room, his legs moving rigidly from the hip sockets as though the knees wouldn't bend.

Mom slowly straightened the papers and finally she stood up, too.

"George, how could you?" she said bitterly, and

without waiting for an answer, followed Dad out of the room.

My eyes met Ollie's. They were large and scared. I wanted to say something to him about how I hoped this would make things easier for him and Jeri, but it sounded too righteous somehow. I crossed the room and started up the stairs where Jeri was still sitting in exactly the same position she'd been before. She was staring up at me, a dazed expression on her face. She drew her legs up tight to let me pass, and I went in my room and lay on my back till it was time for bed.

When the May issue of the school newspaper came out, it carried the names of all the seniors and what they planned to do after graduation:

Marshall Evans, University of Minnesota . . . David Hahn, Oberlin College . . . Bud Irving, Carnegie-Mellon . . . George Richards, work.

SEVEN

I was living at home, with meals provided, but I still felt like a pioneer. It was uncharted territory; nothing had ever happened like this in our family before.

At first I figured I could get by with working funerals at Saunders. After all, I'd been paying my expenses all along, hadn't I? Then I kept track of everything I bought for a week—T-shirt, watchband, pizza, haircut, English Leather deodorant stick, gas, Clearasil, windshield wipers, bowling. . . . I was surprised how much it came to, and I realized I couldn't use Dad's charge accounts anymore. I put off buying some new Adidas sneakers. Put off buying a record album. My old Chevy needed an oil change, so I got that, but what if it needed a tuneup? Then, when Dad handed me the bill for my car insurance instead of paying it himself, I knew I had to be able to count on more than the possibility that someone would be buried over the weekend.

I knew, too, that right now I saw it as a challenge. The old adrenaline was working overtime— me against Dad. When September came, though, and the guys went off to college, I was going to be in limbo. I'd been all set to enter the U. of M. come fall, but once I said I wouldn't, there was no backing down.

I needed a job, a nine-to-five job. I could still do funerals on weekends.

For three days the last week in May, I skipped school to go job hunting. Each morning after the others left, I circled the possibilities in the want ads and started calling.

"Experience?" they all asked. Parking cars for a funeral home didn't seem to count. I was offered a telephone solicitation job, one of those deals where you go down the numbers in the telephone book and try to finish your spiel before they hang up on you. The guy kept telling me how much I could earn and how I could do it in the comfort of my own home. I knew better. I'd hung up on a few myself.

I managed to get two interviews, one with a carpet-cleaning company and the other with a fencing contractor. The carpet man said he'd call me if he decided to take me on, not to call him. And after I'd driven clear over to St. Paul, the fencing contractor said he couldn't hire me because he knew I wouldn't stay—I'd only stick with the job till I went off to college in September.

"I'm not going to college in September," I told him.

He looked me over. "What's your dad do for a living?"

I hesitated. Then I told him.

"Yeah, you're not going to college and I'm the attorney-general," he said. And he waved me out.

By the first of June I still didn't have anything lined up and I was feeling desperate. Discount was lifeguard at the municipal pool; Psycho was working for his uncle; Dave was clerking in a hardware store; and even Jeri had a job, dipping ice cream at Bridgeman's. I told myself I'd say yes to the first place that wanted to hire me.

It was the Green Thumb Garden Center that took me on.

"Well, now, I'll tell you," said the owner. "I'm looking for someone who's willing to do just about anything we've got. A gopher, that's what I need."

I stared at him blankly.

"This is going to be a little different from standing outside a funeral parlor," Mr. Fletcher said.

I nodded.

"I'll start you out at minimum wage, and raise you fifty cents by the end of summer if you stay on. Another fifty by Christmas. You've got to dress in old enough clothes that you can haul fifty-pound sacks of fertilizer off a truck, but not so old you scare the customers if you're working the cash register."

"I'm hired?" I said, scarcely believing.

"Got you down for the day after graduation," he said. "June seventeenth."

"Got a job," I said that night at Psycho's, grinning. "Out at the Green Thumb. Minimum wage, but I get a fifty-cent raise at the end of summer."

"Doing what?" asked Discount.

I tried to remember exactly what Fletcher had told me. "He called it something crazy . . . an animal . . . a groundhog, I think."

Psycho gave me a puzzled look. "A groundhog?"

"He said I'd be doing just about anything they had to do."

"Sure it wasn't a gopher?" asked Discount.

"Yeah! That was it! How'd you know? A gopher!"

Discount and Psycho fell over the bench press, laughing.

"Go-for, you ninny!" Discount yelped. "He means 'go for this,' 'go for that.'"

I felt like a moron, but I also felt good. I was going to show Dad I could make it on my own. Well, almost on my own. From then on, however, I wasn't George anymore. "Gopher," the guys called me.

I didn't wear a 17-inch collar by the week of the prom; it was barely a 16, but I'll admit I looked pretty nice in the tux. Discount, Dave, and I were all going to pick up our dates in separate cars, meet at Murray's Restaurant for dinner, then drive to the prom from there so we'd each have his own car afterward. Psycho, of course, wasn't going. He kept saying all week he'd invited some girl from another school, and the day of the prom he said she was sick. It's a good thing, too, because I bet five dollars he wouldn't show, Dave bet that he would, and Discount bet that he'd show but bring his cousin.

Discount's tux was really awesome—all white, white shoes, the works—with a red cummerbund. Dave had rented a gray tux and a silk top hat, while I chose a midnight blue with tails.

Discount's mom whistled when she went by the door and saw us parading about Bud's room, trying them on.

"You guys are going to knock 'em dead," she told us, and checked to make sure the cuffs came where they were supposed to be, the creases perfect.

Right at that moment I wished I had a mother who would say "knock 'em dead" to me. I couldn't imagine Mom ever saying that; it wasn't in her vocabulary. Dave gave Mrs. Irving a wide smile as she left, and I wondered if he was thinking the same thing. His mom and little sister live across town, and Dave drops by every weekend, but it's not the same as having your mom in the house.

The reason I went to the prom with Maureen Kimball was that I kept comparing every girl to Karen Gunderson, and nobody measured up. There was one girl in homeroom who was a close second, but she had a boyfriend at the University and was taking him. So I asked Maureen. She didn't even act surprised—almost seemed as though she knew I'd take her.

The prom sure put a hole in my budget. The tuxedo rental, the tickets, and the corsage came to a hundred bucks right there. Dinner, another sixty. Every time I turned around, there was something else to buy. Dave said that his dad wanted to take photos of all three couples before the dance, so at least we wouldn't have the expense of photos there at the prom.

That afternoon, after Dave and I had picked up the flowers, we passed a drugstore and Dave slipped inside.

"One more stop," he said, so I ambled in after him. Dave was looking over the assortment of condoms there on a rack next to pipe tobacco.

I stared at him.

"Just want to pick up a box," he said.

I pretended I was looking at the tobacco, but my eyes kept drifting back to the condoms. On every box there was a misty photo of a couple in water. A guy and gal standing in a lake with their arms around each other, kissing. . . . A couple smiling at each other on a sailboat. . . . A man and woman walking out into the surf holding hands. . . . You'd think they were spawning or something. *For feeling in love,* it said on one box. *Golden transparent,* said another. *For her pleasure—the ribbed condom with the lubra-tip.*

I could feel my neck getting hot.

Dave chose two boxes of the golden transparent and plunked them down on the counter. The clerk rang them up without batting an eye. When we got outside, Dave handed one of the boxes to me.

"Live a little," he said.

"I don't think I need that," I told him.

"Well, keep it, just in case," he said. "You never know. Better safe than sorry."

Back in my room, I crammed two condoms behind the driver's license in my wallet. You didn't usually have a wallet with you when you went out in the water with a girl, but I didn't know what else to do with them.

It was warm that night—for Minneapolis, anyway. I was ready by seven-fifteen. Ollie had shined my shoes to such a luster they reflected the dark blue of my tails. I'd washed my car but forgotten to vacuum the inside, so I paid Ollie to do it while I dressed.

"You look very nice," Mom said as I took Maureen's corsage from the refrigerator. Dad aimed a weak smile in my direction.

"Thanks," I said.

She followed me to the door. "Are we going to see Maureen?" she asked tentatively. "Do you want us to take a picture of the two of you?"

"We've got that all arranged," I said. "See you later." I clattered down the steps, grinned at Ollie, who stood holding the car door open, the nozzle of the vacuum in his other hand, and took off.

I didn't especially enjoy driving away without waving at Mom, didn't like not sharing more with my parents. But every time guilt got the best of me and I made some small gesture to patch things up, they seemed cold and distant. Then, after they'd thought better of it and were nice to me in turn, I was mad again and not speaking. We just never seemed to connect.

Maureen was waiting for me at the door, and she didn't even look like the same person. She was wearing a silver dress with the back bare to the waist, little spaghetti straps over the shoulders.

"Wow!" I said appreciatively. Her red hair was piled on top her head except for one long curl that hung down at the side, and there were silver earrings shaped like snowflakes in her ears.

"Like it?" Maureen asked.

"You look great," I told her.

"Have fun, you two," her mother said. Just before we left, Maureen pulled a large wicker basket from the hall closet and handed it to me.

"Picnic," she said, smiling.

I looked at the basket. "I thought I was taking you to dinner."

Maureen tugged impatiently at my arm. "You are, silly. I mean afterward. My treat."

I put her basket in the trunk, and when we got

to Dave's, Bud's car was already there. It didn't occur to me until we were all lined up in front of the mantel, the girls in long dresses, guys behind them, that this was the first time I had ever been in Dave Hahn's living room. First time I'd entered his house.

Mr. Hahn had the camera on a tripod.

"Dave, it's really nice of your dad to do this for us," said his date, a dark-haired girl in a red dress.

"It's his job," Dave said. "He does weddings, bar mitzvahs, commercial photography, you name it. . . ."

And then I realized that Mr. Hahn was a professional photographer. He was a man with a job, a firm, a house, a son. . . . He wasn't just a homosexual. Funny about labels.

"Now if the young lady on the end will move in just a little," Mr. Hahn said, smiling. "That's it. Now the gentleman in the middle—raise your chin just a bit. Good. Perfect!"

Mr. Hahn's male friend was standing in the doorway to the living room holding a cup of coffee, watching the proceedings. He was about the same age as my dad. It occurred to me that he had a job of some kind, too—wasn't just a label.

Mr. Hahn stepped back from the camera, holding a cable release in his hand. "Okay, now, I want you all to think about school, studying, final exams," he intoned.

We all groaned.

"Now think about *sum*-mer!" he said.

We sent up a cheer. The shutter clicked. He took another and another. A picture of the girls together, the guys together, then each couple separately.

83

"Could I order a print of each?" Discount asked him. "I'll be glad to pay."

"It's on the house," said Dave's father. "Glad to do it."

We had a good time at the restaurant. The girls kept teasing Discount about his white tux, insisting there was a gravy stain on the lapel, or that he had caught his sleeve in the butter. Maureen passed up the shrimp cocktail, which helped out my budget, but didn't order the least expensive thing on the menu either, and make me feel like a cheapskate. She was looking more attractive to me all the time.

When we got to the Calhoun Beach Club about ten, it seemed as though the entire senior class had come—all except Psycho, of course. Karen Gunderson was there in a pale green dress that hugged her body, outlining her hip bones, and she and Bob Ellis had eyes only for each other. During the slow numbers, I turned Maureen so I could watch Karen—drink her in with my eyes. It didn't make sense holding one girl in my arms and thinking about another, but some things don't run on logic.

About eleven o'clock, when the band took a break, we went outside and followed some of the couples down to Lake Calhoun. A guy named Wally Baisinger had his dad's boat for the evening, a thirty-two-foot cruiser, and you could look down into the cabin and see where Wally and his date ate their champagne supper before the prom. Wally was inviting some of his friends aboard for a cruise on the lake, and Dave Hahn and his date got on. I took Maureen back to the Beach Club, and we danced a few more numbers.

It was supposed to last till one o'clock, but at midnight, Maureen looked up at me and said, "Let's go. I promised you a picnic."

"Sure you don't want to stay around a little longer?" I asked.

"I'm sure," she said. "What about you?"

"Bring on the picnic," I said.

The place she had in mind was within walking distance, she told me. I got the wicker basket out of the trunk, and we started down the path. Out on the water, we could see the lights of a few boats, and I wondered which one was Wally's.

It was a half-hour's walk, actually, to the place Maureen was going; there was a three-quarters moon that illuminated the way. Maureen held her shoes in her hand and went barefoot. When we reached the fence around Lakewood Cemetery, she said, "This is it." There was even an opening to crawl through.

"You been here before?" I asked her.

"Not with you," came her answer.

Lakewood Cemetery had everything you could want—winding paths, a pond, hilly places, and dark grottoes in the trees. We chose a secluded spot where the damp grass gave way to the crunch of dry pine needles. Maureen sat down and opened her basket.

She'd thought of everything. There was a blanket, a tiny lantern with a candle in it, matches, a bottle of wine, cheese, crackers, olives, strawberries the size of plums, and some kind of lemony cake. There was also a bottle of mosquito repellent.

"Boy, you come prepared!" I laughed. She smiled and spread a cloth on the blanket while I opened the wine.

We could see only well enough to find the food. Maureen's face was just a blur in the shadows, and we sat cross-legged on the blanket across from each other. Now and then leaves rustled somewhere above us or the distant noise of traffic on Lake Street drifted through, but mostly we listened to the sound of our own chewing. I sort of wished we had a radio. Music. Something.

"This was a great idea," I told her.

"It always seems such an anticlimax to go straight home," she said.

We fed each other the olives, then the strawberries. One slipped from my grasp and we laughed as we hunted around on the blanket for it. Sheltered in the thick pines and warmed by the wine, I began to perspire. I took off my jacket and tie. As I looked around for a place to lay them, I saw Maureen slipping out of her dress. She blew out the candle.

"Hey!" I laughed.

"Why not stretch out and be comfortable?" she asked, and lay down on the blanket beside me. I could barely see her. I couldn't even tell if she had on anything at all. I swallowed.

"Well?" she said.

"What?"

"Why not be comfortable?"

My heart began to pound. "Why not?" I said, and took off my shirt and socks. I leaned over and kissed her. She put her hands on the back of my neck and drew me down beside her. I wondered if I'd known all along what was coming. It wasn't as though she were talking me into something I didn't want to do. I reached back into my hip pocket for my wallet. Then I stroked her arms, her neck, her chest, and finally, I just let it happen—just swam with the tide. And when we walked slowly back to the car later, I knew I'd be in that cemetery again with Maureen. If not there, someplace else. I didn't feel especially proud of myself, but I didn't feel guilty either. Just different. Very adult. Easy and uneasy, both at the same time.

The way Mom found out about it was that I told her, more or less. Two weeks after the prom, Dave gave Discount and me a set of the photos his dad had taken, and I left them on our coffee table. Jeri found them after dinner and was looking them over, commenting on the girls' dresses and how I looked like a nerd, the way I was smiling. Then she passed them on to Mom.

"These look like professional photos, George," Mom said. "Who took them?"

"Mr. Hahn." I went down in the basement to get my lifting gloves and came back up, pulling on a T-shirt. Typhus danced around, thinking I was taking her out.

"Dave's father? In their house?"

"Where else?" I said.

Mom laid the photos in her lap. "I thought we had an understanding about your going over there," she told me.

I started toward the door. "If it's my sexual identity," I said, "you can stop worrying about that now."

"Meaning . . . ?" Mother asked.

"Figure it out for yourself," I said, quoting Grandpa Richards, and drove on over to Psycho's.

EIGHT

Crack. Crunch. I had lined up my parents' values —the wise and the foolish, the good and the ridiculous—and was stomping on them one by one. The more important a rule was to them, the less important it became to me. I didn't enjoy hurting them, it wasn't that, but I had a statement to make, and I didn't know how else to do it.

Graduation was pretty awkward. Aunt Sylvia and Uncle Lawrence came down from Duluth, and Grandpa Richards drove over to attend the ceremony. We all sat out in the back yard later, just as we'd done after Trish's graduation, but nobody knew what to talk about. With Trish, the talk had been of Cornell, where she'd be going to college, and how lucky she was to get in. The Green Thumb Garden Center didn't evoke the same enthusiasm somehow.

What upset everyone, I guess, was that all these years Gramps had been saving his gold wristwatch to give to me. He had worn it through Harvard Law School before Dad was born, had worn it for his bar exam, worn it when he argued his first case, and during all the years in his law firm. When he retired, he put the watch away and said he would present it to his first grandson, which was me, on the occasion of his high school graduation. He had envisioned me going to college with it, not wearing it to haul fifty-pound bags of fertilizer off a truck.

"Thanks, Gramps. It's really beautiful!" I'd said when I opened the box. "I'll save it for special occasions."

Gramps just nodded and turned away, drumming his fingers on the arm of the lawn chair.

Aunt Sylvia and Uncle Lawrence presented me with a check for fifty dollars. Mom and Dad's gift, however, had been inside an envelope that I'd found on my plate at breakfast. There was a card with the traditional "To our son on his graduation" message, but on the inside flap Dad had written, "Your graduation gift from us is the same we gave Patricia: our agreement to pay all college expenses, including graduate, law, or medical school, when, and if, you decide to continue your education. Love, Dad and Mom."

I'd folded the card up again, stuck it back in the envelope, and drunk my orange juice. I hadn't even said thank you. Somehow I got the message that accomplishments to date didn't matter; just being *me* didn't matter; I wasn't going to get a reward until I danced to their tune.

"What was in the envelope, George?" Ollie had asked me later when I went upstairs for my cap and gown.

"A bribe," I'd told him, and went on out to the car.

Now we sat around the back yard drinking lemonade, waiting for dinner time, watching Typhus scratch herself there in the grass. There just didn't seem to be all that much to talk about, to me, anyway.

"Well, George, I understand you're going to be working in the garden center," Aunt Sylvia said finally. "That's certainly something different, isn't it?"

"Yeah, I guess so," I told her, trying desperately to think of something more interesting to say.

Uncle Lawrence sucked on his pipe. "I'll bet all that weight-lifting you've been doing will come in handy when you haul around bags of mulch," he said, smiling.

"I suppose so." I laughed. "You ought to check out Ollie sometime, though. He's starting to build some muscle, too."

Nobody picked up the ball. There was silence for a long time.

"When do you start?" Grandpa Richards asked finally.

"Tomorrow."

"How nice," said Aunt Sylvia.

We all lapsed back into silence again. Jeri managed to go into the house for ice and didn't come back. A little later I could hear her stereo playing softly upstairs. Ollie was lying in the hammock in his best clothes, one leg hanging over the side, rocking with his foot. I sat in a deck chair off to one side, head tipped back, staring up at the sky through the web of branches, Grandpa's watch feeling heavy and unfamiliar on my wrist.

"How are things going at *your* school?" Aunt Sylvia asked Mom, since Ollie's schoolwork wasn't a fit topic of conversation either, and Jeri had disappeared.

"Oh, the usual," said Mother. "It's night school

that's getting me down. I'm taking six hours this semester, and I hardly have time to think."

"Do you really need a master's degree?" Aunt Sylvia wanted to know.

"If I want a promotion, I do," Mom told her.

"Promoted to what?" Uncle Lawrence asked.

"Principal, maybe. Administrative supervisor. Paperwork and committee meetings, that's what I'll be promoted to. Ironical, isn't it? Take a step up the ladder, and you're promoted right out of the classroom."

I felt like an eavesdropper, somehow, sitting back there in the deck chair, eyes on the sky. Slowly I raised my head and looked at Mom. She was staring down at her lap, smoothing the wrinkles from her dress.

"You've always loved teaching," Aunt Sylvia reminded.

"I know, but all these young teachers coming in now have master's degrees," Mom said. "I'm going to find myself being supervised by a person half my age unless I have that darn M.A. after my name."

There was hurt and humiliation in Mom's voice. She could have been almost anybody talking— a girl who hadn't made the hockey team, a college student who had been passed over by the sororities. . . . Somehow, I'd never thought of her as anything other than a capable, self-confident woman. She was simply a science teacher, Dad was a lawyer, and that was that. Funny about labels. . . .

I looked down at the gold watch on my wrist and thought about Gramps when he was a young man, sweating over his bar exam. I wondered if the worries you had back when you were in your teens and twenties traveled right along with you through life—if somehow, though your body grew older—some part of you stayed the same insecure kid that Ollie was right now.

Life's weird, I told myself.

When I walked in the door of the Green Thumb Garden Center, I thought I had entered a tropical rain forest. There was a constant dripping sound that came from freshly watered plants. Baskets of begonias hung from the low rafters, the only flower I recognized because Mom has a begonia plant on our porch. A giant rubber tree stood in one corner. There were plants before, behind, beside, and below me. The room had a humid, lush feeling about it, like wet concrete and mud after a rain.

I wandered about through the plants, listening to the murmur of voices that came from outside somewhere, then entered a large well-lit room filled with pottery, vases, Miracle-Gro, Sheep Stix, and the ceramic elves, rabbits, and Mexican burros that some people plant in their front yards.

"George Richards?"

I whirled around. A large man came through a side door carrying a box of pink flamingoes, the kind that stand on one leg next to the driveway and, when the wind blows, their wings whirl around like propellers. He put the box on the counter and shook my hand. "I'm Jack Fletcher," he said. "Glad to see you're on time. I appreciate a fellow coming to work when he's supposed to. Let me show you around."

I followed him outside.

The Green Thumb Garden Center spread out in all directions behind the building itself. Small trees, their roots bundled in burlap, leaned against a greenhouse. On either side of the dirt road, which rose up and over a small hill, were row after row of flowering bushes, a rainbow of pink, orange, and yellow. I wondered if any of the bouquets at Saunders Funeral Home had come from a place called The Green Thumb. Sort of macabre, when you think about it.

"Any questions you have about the work you do outside," Fletcher said, "you ask me." He swept one large arm in the direction of the hill, the road, and the greenhouse. "Any problems you have *inside*, you ask Shirl. She takes care of the shop. Come on and we'll meet her. Shirl!" he bellowed, pushing open the door.

I followed him inside once more. He was a large man, his back the size of a refrigerator, his skin brown and leathery from a perennial tan. He strode across the concrete floor of the shop, his huge galoshes unbuckled and flopping on his feet.

"Shirl!" he yelled again.

This time a woman came out of the small office adjoining the shop. She was probably thirty, but wore her hair fluffy and loose, and was dressed in a checked blouse and denim skirt.

"Shirl, this is our new employee, George Richards. George, Shirley King."

"Nice to meet you, George." She extended her hand, and her nails were twice as long as mine, the color of copper. Her face stretched into a smile, and little wrinkles formed at the corners of her eyes. Maybe she was older than thirty.

"I've got to talk with a customer about landscaping," Mr. Fletcher said to her, "so you show George the ropes in here. We'll start him out in the shop."

"Fine," Shirl said, and smiled some more, then added, "I don't want to hear any of that 'Mrs. King' business, now. Makes me feel so old you wouldn't believe."

"Okay," I grinned.

She wasn't the best teacher I've ever had. Every time she started to tell me one thing, she'd interrupt herself and tell me something else, so it ended up that I knew a little about a lot of things but not a lot about anything.

Shirley stopped talking suddenly. "I'm confusing you, aren't I? Tell you what, why don't you start out with the dusting. That way, at least, you'll learn what's on the shelves and where." She produced a feather duster from under the counter and I went to work on the cans of Miracle-Gro and the Mexican burros. Stepping backward at the end of one row, I bumped into something, and almost fell. Turning around, I saw a plastic wishing well with about a foot of water in it, the bottom covered with nickels and pennies.

"Easy money," Shirl said as she passed. "You'd be amazed how many of those we sell in a month, George. People put them out in their front yards, would you believe?"

"You just put money in it and leave it there?" I asked.

Her eyes crinkled with laughter again. "*We* don't put in a cent. Customers come in, see a wishing well, and next thing you know they're digging around in their pockets for change. Kids beg their mothers for a penny. You ever want to make some quick money, George, you set something out in your front yard and fill it with water. I swear, you could put an old commode out by the sidewalk and folks would be dropping change in it."

We laughed.

When six o'clock came, I didn't feel I'd done very much, but after a few days, I'd gotten a taste of several different jobs. There were two other people working part-time—Harvey, somewhat retarded, who helped load the truck, and Anne, about my age, who helped out in the shop. I was glad whenever Anne came on duty, because then I could work outside, and I liked that best—digging up bushes, wrapping the roots, and loading them on a truck. I learned what to water and how much, where to set the sprinklers. Took my turn at the cash register, too, and even learned to wrap a bouquet for delivery, tie it with ribbon.

I couldn't figure Shirl out, though. Every day about three, she'd go into the back room and call her daughter. Heather was her name. Fifth grade. Called to see if she got home okay. The kid was going to some kind of special day camp—gymnastics or something. Every day it was the same. Shirley would call home, wait till Heather answered, and say, "Hi, Sweetie! How many hearts did you break today?"

I could tell by the way Shirl said it that she'd been saying it every day. Since first grade? Third? All Heather's life, maybe? How's the little kid whose Mom thinks she's about the most gorgeous child in the universe? What do you say to a mom who assumes that boys are jumping off of bridges from unrequited love? How do you ever tell her that maybe, on the contrary, it's *your* heart that's breaking, that you *don't* always get the attention she thinks you deserve?

I didn't know why I was worrying about the emotional health of some little girl I'd never seen. Maybe I was thinking about Ollie. It was good, though, to be a part of the team there at the Green Thumb. It was a place to go to every day, a regular paycheck every two weeks. I could still work funerals at Saunders on Sundays, so my bank account was growing. I started paying Mom something every week for room and board—just to show I could do it. She was surprised. So was Dad. I had proved I wasn't just bumming around. We all wanted to keep communication going between us, so things grew more polite around our house, but I couldn't really say they got any warmer.

Just as I knew I would, I continued to see Maureen Kimball. It was pretty heady stuff, lying there on a blanket in Lakewood Cemetery with Maureen beside me, skin against skin. Once we'd started what we had, it was hard to stop. I was buying rubbers regularly now and hiding them in my saxophone case in the closet. I'd make out with Maureen in the evening and think a lot about her the next day—about how it was—the next four or five days, in fact, until I saw her again. Except that it wasn't Maureen so much I was thinking about; it was sex. And the sex just happened to be with Maureen, that's all.

I was dying to tell the guys, but I didn't. Something held me back. Dave Hahn told me what *he* did the night of the prom, though—about taking his girl into the stateroom of the Baisinger's cabin cruiser—about how she was wearing this gown with straps that crossed in back and how he had a devil of a time getting her out of it. I listened. I laughed. I mean, what do you expect?

"Happy?" Maureen said once as we snuggled there on the blanket.

"Umm," I said.

She lay beside me twisting the hair on my chest, and I'd wished there was more to twist. I was glad for the lifting I'd done at Psycho's. If you don't have a lot of hair on your chest, it helps to have some muscle.

"*I* am," Maureen told me.

You never know about girls, though. I mean, was she *really* happy? Or did she just say she was happy so I'd think I'd taken her to paradise, which would make *me* so happy I'd fall in love with her, which would make *her* delirious? Sometimes it's better not to think too hard about it. Sometimes it's better just to say "umm" and let it go.

Wonder of wonders, things seemed to be going better in our family. Mom and Dad left me alone, and I didn't bother them. If we didn't talk, we didn't fight; so we didn't say much to each other. Trish and Roger were out of school for the summer and had rented a cottage on Cape Cod for a week. Trish wrote that they were having a marvelous time. Ollie was feeling good because he was out of school for the summer too, and whenever there wasn't a funeral at Saunders on Sundays, I'd take him swimming at Lake Harriet or camping or out in the woods somewhere to work on his orienteering merit badge for Scouts. People in Minnesota make the most of summer, they get so little of it.

"I want to be a forest ranger," Ollie told me once when we were charting a 12-point orienteering course, our maps spread out across the table. "Man, that's what I'd *really* like to do."

"So *do* it!" I said.

Ollie just looked at me. I knew what he was thinking. Not that he couldn't make it; he couldn't make it past the folks, that's what.

Ollie was growing taller. Skinnier and taller. We kept working with him over at Psycho's, and he did okay on the weights, but all his pounds seemed to go into height.

"Feel, George," he'd say every so often, and stick his arm out, and I'd squeeze his biceps. I told him not to go measuring himself, though. You can go nuts measuring yourself. Your chest, especially. Hard to measure a chest. Tape slips a quarter of an inch, off a rib or something, and you've just lost three-quarters of an inch.

We didn't see much of Jeri. She worked four afternoons a week, and weekends she was off somewhere with her girlfriends. When she was home, she was either in her room or lying out on a towel in the backyard baking, headphones on, feet wiggling in time to the music. Whenever Mom asked her to do something, she'd get up and do it and go back to the towel. I mean, she was with us and she wasn't.

It was about the middle of July. After I'd taken Maureen to the movies, we made love in the backseat of the car, which isn't exactly easy or comfortable if you want the truth, but it was raining out. It was getting so I couldn't wait to get the preliminaries out of the way—the movie or concert or whatever—just so we could have sex. And because that was really about all I was interested in with Maureen, I knew I'd have to break it off. Maybe that's why I didn't tell the guys I'd scored—so I wouldn't have to explain to them when it was over. About the time I'd decide to do it, though—to tell her—she'd rest one hand on my leg or something, and I'd think, just one more time, and we'd coast on into the next week.

On this night, though, after I got home, I kept thinking about Maureen and wondering if she knew how I felt about her; how I *didn't* feel about her. That was more to the point. It was almost twelve forty-five—maybe one o'clock—and I was listening to the rain on the trees outside—a low sort of hiss, droplets falling from the eaves—when I saw the slow sweep of headlights on the ceiling as a car turned the corner. I heard the hum of the motor as it drove down the block, then the soft purr of the engine as it stopped and the motor cut off.

Then I heard something else—the creak of floorboards out in the hall. I lifted my head, listening. It was so quiet, I wondered if I'd imagined it. Jeri's door had been closed when I came home, the signal that she was in, so I'd turned off the lamp. Maybe somehow she'd opened the front door so quietly I hadn't heard, and was just now coming up.

Then, however, I heard the stairs creak, and I knew that Jeri was going down, not up. Softly, so softly that no one else in the house could have noticed, the front door opened, then clicked shut again. I heard a car door open, a car door close. Then a motor started up.

I rolled over and looked out the window. A car was moving slowly down the street with its head-lights off.

NINE

I don't know what time Jeri got home that night. When I got up the next morning, her door was closed.

It wasn't until later, when I was mowing the grass, that I asked her about it. She was stretched out on a towel like an Egyptian princess, worshipping the sun, and made no move to leave, even when the Toro came within three feet of her head. I turned the mower off.

"What shall I trim first?" I asked. "Your hair or your toenails?"

Jeri took off her sunglasses and glared at me. "Ha, ha," she said and sat up, gathering her lotion and sandals and magazines.

I studied her, one hand on the mower. "What time did you get in this morning?" I asked.

She looked up at me as though about to protest that I had come in last, then stopped. "How did you know?" she asked finally.

"Never mind how I knew."

"I suppose you've blabbed to Mom."

"I haven't said anything to anybody. But who do you know that you have to go sneaking around with? That marine you met at the 18-20 Club?"

Jeri frowned as though she couldn't remember. "Oh, him!" she said. "He was a jerk." She stood up and folded her towel.

"Who was it, then?"

"Just some guy I met!" Jeri said. "Since when did you get so interested in my life?"

"You'd better be careful, Jeri," I told her.

"Look who's talking," she said.

That was the pattern of conversations between Jeri and me—each of us trying to guess what the other knew. I watched her flounce off indignantly toward the house.

"My ex-husband," said Shirley King, "didn't know dandelions from daisies. When it came to doing things in the yard or around the house, he was a total zero. He wouldn't change a lightbulb if I didn't ask, and even then he'd want to know if we really needed it."

We had received a new shipment of ceramic lawn ornaments called Lawnimals—cutesy little animals who all seemed to have evolved from Bambi. Hens and chickens, cats that clung to the side of your house, deer that smiled innocently at traffic from your evergreens, pelicans that could double as newspaper receptacles, and skunks with their tails all poised. Would you believe we had customers who came in and bought one of each?

I was opening the crates, and Shirley was checking the animals over for damage. When Shirl started talking about her ex, though, she always had to do everything twice because she never paid attention the first time around.

"Oh, lord, what *is* that?" she gasped, as I pulled out a bile-green frog with protruding eyes, and then, without missing a beat, she went on: "He always said if you let something alone, it would fix itself. Television was fuzzy, I'd ask him could he please wiggle the antenna, and he'd say, 'Don't touch it; it'll fix itself.' A lamp get to flickering, he'd say, 'Don't touch it, Shirl. It'll stop.' "

"Hey, Shirley," I said, "you're putting those price stickers on upside down."

"Darn," she said. She reached for the bile-green frog and put the price sticker over one eyeball. "You know what he said the day I told him our marriage was going down the tube?"

" 'Don't worry, it'll fix itself'?" I guessed.

"You got it. I walked out with Heather, and I don't think he even noticed for a week."

"So now he has to take care of the house by himself?" I asked.

"Are you kidding? He didn't know how to turn on one blessed thing except the TV. He moved out a month later and put it up for sale. So now Heather and I are on our own." She waited.

"I'll bet you're doing all right, too," I said, as I began stacking the frogs on a lower shelf where they wouldn't be so visible.

"Are you kidding?" Shirl said again, and gave me a look.

She brought Heather into the shop one afternoon on their way to the dentist. I couldn't believe that this was the kid who was supposed to be breaking hearts every day. She was a ten-year-old girl with no indentations whatsoever from her shoulders to her feet. She had a round plain face draped on either side by long straight hair that refused to turn up at the ends, even for a moment. She was also shy to the point of pathology. Every

103

time I said something to her, she smiled slightly and stared down at the floor.

Shirl ran her hand through Heather's hair.

"Isn't she a doll?" she said.

"How's day camp, Heather?" I asked.

Heather smiled at her feet.

"Gymnastics, isn't it?"

She nodded.

"You pretty good at it?"

She didn't answer.

"She's terrific!" said Shirl.

I was beginning to feel at home at the Green Thumb—knew what to do when Fletcher wasn't there to tell me. I could check the due dates on all the receipts and make out a delivery schedule that would route the van efficiently around the city—load it so that the shrubs being delivered first were just inside the door. Once when Fletcher strained his back and couldn't come in for two days, Shirl and I managed by ourselves, with a little help from Harvey and Anne.

"You're working out pretty good here, George," Fletcher told me the beginning of August. "Not going to disappoint me and go off to college, are you? The old gopher job's not getting you down?"

"I like the job," I told him. "Lots of variety."

Fletcher kept me on the run, and that was just the way I liked it—no time to think about September and how I'd feel then. Go deliver a holly bush in St. Paul; pick up a dead maple in Burnsville and plant a new one in its place; take a package to the post office; pick up some mailing tape; take the van in for a brake check; drive Harvey home when it rained.

I liked all the people there. Harvey, an oddly shaped man of indeterminate age, sort of rolled his tongue around in his mouth a few times as though tasting every word before he let it go. He had a droll sense of humor if you waited him out. Most people didn't. They listened long enough to get the gist of what he wanted to say, then finished the sentence for him.

Anne was the one who was growing on me. When I first met her, she didn't strike me as anything special—maybe because I saw her in contrast to Shirley. Where Shirley wore mascara and blush and gold bracelets up and down both arms, Anne came to work in a T-shirt and jeans, her hair pulled back with a scarf or rubber band or whatever, it seemed, was handy. It was almost as though she didn't want to be noticed. But after a while, working around her, I realized that she didn't have to do anything at all to get attention. She had the sort of eyes that dance when she looked at you, like there were all kinds of things she might say that she wouldn't. Alive. Really alive. I began to look forward to the days Fletcher assigned me to work in the shop with her. Which made it all the more difficult to decide what to do about Maureen.

At Saunders one Sunday, I was standing outside in my suit and tie, perspiration pouring down my face, when Dave came around the building.

"Man!" he said, "I'm going to hang out here for a while. There's not a bit of shade around in back."

"The service just started," I told him. "You've got time to cool off."

He came up the steps and we both resumed the standard funeral-home stance, hands clasped behind our backs, legs apart.

"Some of the guys are coming over Saturday night for poker," Dave told me. "You want to come by?"

"Sure. What time?"

"Nine, maybe."

"I'll be there."

I could tell, even though Dave was staring straight ahead, that he was smiling. I figured he was going to ask me about Maureen—ask if I'd miss seeing her that night—but he didn't. He asked something else.

"Remember back in seventh grade," he said, "when I'd ask you to come over and you couldn't?"

"Yeah," I told him. Now I knew what the question was.

"Your folks?" he said.

"Yeah."

"Well, they weren't the only ones."

"I figured as much," I told him. "Sort of silly, wasn't it?"

He only shrugged. A car pulled in the drive, and Dave directed it to the parking lot behind the building.

"You know . . ." he said, and paused, as though maybe he wasn't going to say it after all, then barreled on ahead. ". . . when Dad . . . came 'out of the closet' . . . *you* know . . ."

I waited again.

"Well, it wasn't just him who had a hard time of it, it was all of us—the whole family. Like we'd been shut up in the closet with him. It wasn't just what he was going to tell people about this friend of his, it was what *we* were going to tell *our* friends."

I stole a glance at Dave. "Pretty rough, huh?"

"Dad said he was tired of pretending to be something he wasn't, that being gay was just the way he was, like the color of his eyes or something. But the rest of us went right on pretending because we didn't know what else to do."

"You wish he hadn't then? Come out?"

Dave was quiet a moment. "At first I felt that way, because it was pulling the family apart. I admired him for his courage and hated his guts, both at the same time. As long as he'd been willing to keep the friend separate, out of sight, Mom was willing to live the lie. But once he went public, Mom left. I decided to stay, though, because I just couldn't see us all walking out on him, you know? But Mom and Dad are still friends. Weird, isn't it?"

"Life's weird," I said in reply. That was getting to be my favorite phrase.

We played poker at Dave's house on Saturday, and his dad played, too. His dad cleaned us out, in fact, but we were only using chips so it didn't matter. When we put a nickel ante on the chips, we wouldn't let Mr. Hahn play, so he went out in the kitchen and made us egg rolls from scratch. The aroma of pork and onions and sesame oil wafted into the dining room.

I thought about Dave that week—thought about all the girls he'd made it with, probably to show he wasn't gay. Then I got to thinking about his father wanting people to accept him like he was; about Ollie wanting to be a forest ranger—about as far from Spanish as he could get; about me not wanting to go to Harvard; about Mom wishing that she could get promoted and still stay in the classroom—a teacher. Seemed like all of life's problems could be boiled down to people just wanting to *be*—to be what was best for them. And I wondered why it was so difficult, anyway.

TEN

We all turned eighteen over the summer—Dave and Marsh and I. This made us eligible, along with Bud, for the 18-20 Club, but once I knew I could go, it lost its appeal. I'd thought of taking Maureen there in hopes of pairing her off with somebody else. Then I got a better idea: Get her interested in Marshall Evans. Psycho was big, he was brawny, he was handsome—a lot better-looking than me. Both he and Maureen were going to the University of Minnesota in the fall, and they'd have a lot in common. All I had to do, I figured, was give them a chance to get acquainted. Not that I expected instant miracles. But if Maureen ever latched onto Psycho the way she latched onto me, he'd be in heaven.

Marsh was okay with guys, but around girls, he became excruciatingly shy—one big silent lump of mashed potato.

"I don't know what to talk about," he'd confessed once.

"Say *anything,* Psycho!" we told him. "Smile at the girl and say the first thing that enters your head."

"They'd arrest me," said Marsh.

"Ask questions," I suggested. "That'll get a girl talking about herself and the heat will be off you."

We tried coaching from the sidelines. We tried setting him up with friends of friends. Psycho always ducked out at the last minute. I figured that what Marsh needed was a girl who came on strong, and what better person than Maureen Kimball.

"Marsh," I said when I called him, "you busy tonight?"

"No," said Psycho.

"Meet us at Nilsson's about eight. If you get there first, grab a booth. Okay?"

"Sure," said Psycho.

He didn't ask who the "us" was, so I didn't tell him. If his mind traveled along the same old rut and he was expecting Dave and Discount, that was his problem. Nilsson's was about the last soda fountain drugstore in Minneapolis with a marble-topped counter and booths where you could get a shake, and it was a favorite place to meet on Friday nights while you were deciding where to go after.

"Where we going?" Maureen said when I picked her up. She was wearing a sort of loose sundress without any bra, and you could see little dark circles in front where her breasts brushed up against the material.

"Thought maybe we'd drop by Nilsson's and get some ice cream," I said.

"I couldn't possibly eat a thing," Maureen told me, stretching one arm across the back of the seat and draping her hand over my shoulder.

"Well, I'm starved," I said. "Split a sundae with me."

Maureen fondled my ear. "I'll feed your hungers." She laughed.

I never could figure her out. Maureen wasn't what I'd call wild. She may have slept with a guy or two before me, but if she did, she kept it to herself. I think she really liked me, and decided to do whatever it took to keep me. She never asked what I did when I wasn't with her—didn't want to scare me away, I guess. She was just always, totally available, and that was the problem. God, though, what she could do for Psycho!

I purposely got to Nilsson's late so that Marsh would be in a booth. Through the window I could see him sitting there, checking his watch, then leaning forward, his massive arms on the table, furtively eyeing a couple of girls in the next booth.

"Hey, Psycho!" I said, as though I'd never expected meeting him there. "How you doing?" I slid onto the seat across from him, and Maureen sat down beside me.

Marsh stared at us, his eyes sort of glazing over when he saw Maureen. You could hear him swallow.

"You know Maureen, don't you?" I asked.

She answered for him. "Sure. We've seen each other around school."

Psycho managed a faint smile and went on staring somewhere beyond our heads.

"You ordered yet?" I asked him. "I'm going to have the Gold Rush Sundae."

"I just ate," said Psycho. "At home, I mean."

"Well, why don't we order two sundaes, and

you can split one with Maureen, since she's not very hungry either," I suggested. I knew I was pushing it.

The waitress turned in our direction and before we could discuss it further, Psycho bleated, "Coke for me." Maureen said she only wanted a glass of water and I ordered my sundae. When the waitress left, we lapsed into embarrassed silence.

"Guess what?" I said suddenly. "Both of you are going to the University this fall. Talk about coincidence!"

"Us and about eighty-five others from our graduating class," Maureen said dryly. She looked at Psycho. "Have you registered yet?"

"No," he told her.

"What date did you get for orientation?"

"August second."

"Hey! Me, too!" said Maureen.

Psycho looked down at his hands.

Come on, buddy! I pleaded under my breath. Pick up the ball! Run with it!

Marsh looked up suddenly and fastened his eyes on Maureen, his neck a strange shade of pink. "You ever do any weight-lifting?" he asked.

I could almost feel my lungs deflate. Almost feel the smile that crept across Maureen's face.

"No," she said, "I never did."

Across the table, the pink spread to Marshall's cheeks, his ears.

Our order came, and while Maureen and I passed my spoon back and forth between us, I tried to keep up a steady banter. I told Maureen about how many pounds Psycho could bench, how many squats he could do, but she just kept digging away at my caramel syrup and all the while Psycho's Coke was getting lower and lower in his glass. I had to do something.

"Wait right here," I said. "Just remembered I was supposed to call Dad and tell him something about the car."

Maureen slid her legs to one side and I inched past her and over to the phones on the other side of the store.

Wedged in the phone booth behind Dr. Sholl's foot remedies, I held the receiver against my ear and listened to the dial tone, studying the second-hand of Gramp's gold watch. I forced myself to stay in the booth for a full five minutes. All I wanted to do was give them a couple minutes together—let Psycho find out there was at least one girl he could talk to. Secretly, I was hoping that some irresistible urge would rise up in Maureen and she would see in Marsh a challenge—a mountain of muscle just waiting to be conquered.

When the five minutes were up, I put the receiver back, stepped outside the booth, and slowly raised my head above the bunion pads.

Maureen was sitting alone at the table, studying her nails, and Psycho was standing over by the magazine rack, thumbing through a copy of *Newsweek*, his face fever-red. Before I could get over there, he put the magazine back, gave Maureen a slight nod of his head, and barged on outside.

"Where's Marsh?" I asked Maureen.

"The poor guy!" she said. "He got up about ten seconds after you did, George. He's a basket case if I ever saw one. Do me a favor; if we ever come here again, don't let's sit with Marshall Evans."

113

Psycho was pretty sore about what happened at Nilsson's.

"What the hell was I supposed to think?" he asked. "She's your girl!"

"Hey, I told you we were all going out to a movie, didn't I?" I said. I was lying, and Marsh knew it, and that made it worse.

"No, you didn't say a thing about Maureen. You didn't say you were bringing a girl with tits showing right through her dress. There wasn't even a safe place I could look."

"Well, jeez, Marsh, she wasn't going to bite you. You're going to be seeing her around the University. What's the big deal?"

"What's the big deal is right! How come Discount and Dave didn't show? It's like you were trying to push her off on me."

"Oh, come off it, Psycho," I said, but I knew he had me. I also knew that what I'd done only made Marsh feel worse about himself—made it look as though he were so bad off he needed help.

Maybe I was trying to punish myself for it, I don't know, but when I went to work on Monday, I smashed my hand—got my fingers caught between the wheelbarrow and a cinderblock wall.

I told Shirl that the scrape wasn't as bad as it looked, but she insisted on washing my hand in soap and water and bandaging it up, her long fingers with the copper-colored nails holding my palm very gently while she patted it dry.

"Hey, Shirl, it's not amputated or anything," I protested, as she wrapped it in layer after layer of gauze. Anne passed the door of the office, and

I saw her smile as she went by. I shifted impatiently.

"Hold still," Shirl said. "I'm not about to let this get infected and have you sue us or something."

"Fat chance," I told her.

"What were you laughing at?" I asked Anne later as I helped her move the perennials over to the sale table. I had to carry each plant with the palm of my right hand.

"Just the way Shirley was going about it." Anne grinned. "You've got enough gauze there to wrap a belly dancer."

I laughed, too. "I'll take it off when I get home. Got to keep the she-boss happy, though."

"Yeah, I know what you mean," said Anne.

I found myself searching Anne's fingers as she worked, trying to see if she were wearing an engagement ring or something; someone's class ring on a chain around her neck, maybe. She wasn't. She stopped once and held her hair up off the back of her neck, fanning herself with a garden brochure.

"It's so hot!" she said. "For two cents I'd sit down in the wishing well over there."

I reached in my jeans for pennies, and she laughed.

"I'm going swimming after I leave today," she said. "It'll wait."

"Want some company?"

"You can't. Your hand, remember." She walked over to the corner table to rearrange the geraniums and I followed.

"I'll take off the bandage," I said.

She just smiled and shook her head. "I'm meeting some girlfriends."

"Some other time?" I persisted.

"Maybe," she told me.

There was something different about our house that evening. It took me a minute or two to figure it out. Then I realized that there was music coming from the living room and it wasn't the stereo. It was Jeri playing the piano, which she does on rare occasions. Classical music. Like everything else Jeri did, she played well. Except that Trish had done everything well first, so what Jeri accomplished was no big deal around our house.

Mom and Dad sat waiting.

"I almost hate to call her," Mom said. "It's been so long since she's played."

"Well, let her be, then," Dad suggested. "A little dinner music might be nice."

It's strange, sometimes, the difference one person can make in a family. Jeri deciding to play the piano instead of shutting herself up in her room, for example. Even Dad's "pass the butter" seemed more mellow.

"What happened to your hand, George?" Mom asked, and because there was real concern in her voice, I answered civilly:

"Smashed it against a wall with a wheelbarrow. It's not as bad as it looks." I reached for the corn and rolled it around on my plate in a thin puddle of melting butter. Mom started to say something else, but right then Jeri flubbed a couple of notes and ran her hands disgustedly across the keys before she shuffled on into the dining room.

"Why couldn't Chopin have written everything in the key of C?" she asked plaintively, plopping down in her chair.

Mom and Dad laughed. Ollie too. Even grumpy old me managed a smile.

"Why couldn't *War and Peace* be written in half the number of pages?" said Mom, carrying the joke a step further.

It's sort of a family tradition at our house. Somebody starts something ridiculous, and the others try to carry it along. Ollie jumped in with both feet. "Why can't a basketball net be three feet lower?"

Dad was not to be outdone. "Why couldn't Form 1040 be answered true or false?" he said, and that got another burst of laughter.

I wished I had something funny to contribute, but nothing special came to mind. What I was really thinking, though, was how there *were* good times in our family. I wondered why all the faults seemed to rise up lately and smack me between the eyes—as though I had to focus on those in order to get up enough steam to break away.

I was lying on the blanket, staring up at the odd-shaped patches of sky that gleamed through the tangled silhouette of branches. The woods were still in the late afternoon except for the occasional rustle of a squirrel overhead and the faraway drone of cicadas.

Maureen rolled over and put one arm around my neck.

"Hey, lover," she said. I lifted my head and brushed my lips against her cheek, then lay back again. For a moment I felt a stirring of tenderness toward Maureen, not the nothingness I'd been feeling for the past several weeks. Maybe it all

117

had to do with whether I was upside down or right side up, I thought. Wouldn't it be crazy if all life's problems could be solved just by lying on your back? But I knew better. This was it. Maureen had said in the car that she was thinking about going on the Pill. I couldn't let her see a doctor and get a prescription just for me—then walk out on her. It was now or never.

She probed at my ribs with one finger. I grabbed her hand and held it.

"What are you thinking right now?" she asked.

"Everything and nothing," I said finally, which was as loaded an answer as there ever was.

She must have sensed something, because she took her arm off my chest and laid back down beside me, not quite touching.

"What's wrong, George?"

"I'm not really sure," I told her, trying to figure out how to say it.

She ran one hand along my leg. "Something *I* can't cure?"

"Yep." I smiled. "Something not even you can cure." I could tell, however, that *she* wasn't smiling.

"I began to suspect that . . . when you didn't want to make love today."

I sat up. "Sometimes I even surprise myself," I said. "I've just been thinking about us, and feel we ought to start seeing other people, Maureen. You're going to be meeting new guys at the University—they'll ask you out . . . ." Big, magnanimous me.

I could tell it was a line she'd heard before. Girls had even used it on me. When you want to break up, you focus on all the potential dates your partner could get. Mr. Generous here.

Maureen just looked at me. "Maybe I don't *want* to date anyone else, George."

"You ought to be free, though, Maureen, just in case," I told her.

Maureen took the cue and stood up, so I got up too, and together we folded the blanket. She picked up the picnic basket we'd scarcely opened. The sandwiches had gone untouched.

"So who is she?" Maureen asked finally as we started back to the car. "You can tell me. There weren't any strings attached." I glanced over at her. Her lips were pressed bravely together. There was a flatness in her voice, however, that matched the way I felt. I was lower than low.

"Nobody yet. But I want to feel free to date other people, and you deserve the same. That's hard to do when . . . we're as close as we've been."

"It bothers you that you're not going to college this fall. Is that it?" she asked. "That I'll be a student again and you won't? It's *okay*, George, really! That doesn't bother me."

I knew I had to be more specific. If Maureen thought that college was the problem, she'd drop out just to make me feel better. If I wanted to end the relationship once and for all, I had to say so. Sort of.

"It's more than that, Maureen," I told her. "It's really over between us, that's all." Don't make me say anything else, I thought. Don't make me spell it out. How does a guy ever say I don't care for you as much as I should? He doesn't.

She didn't make me say it. Her eyes finally told me that she knew. She moved ahead of me where the path narrowed. Her step was a little too brisk and deliberate, and I felt a rush of guilt that rose,

119

then receded. We didn't talk all the way back to her house. In her driveway, however, she put one hand on top of mine.

"Well, George, it's been fun," she said at last. "Maybe we both need a change. So good-bye, good luck, and all that sort of thing."

Casual to the last. Even Maureen had trouble being herself, I was thinking. But it was easier this way.

"I'll see you around," I said. And that was it.

ELEVEN

There was only one funeral at Saunders on Sunday, so I worked the afternoon shift, then took Ollie to a movie—*The Revenge of the Termite People,* Ollie's choice.

"Wait till you see the scene where the termites gnaw through a wooden coffin to get at a corpse!" Ollie said. "It'll gross you out!"

"I thought you hadn't seen this movie!" I protested.

"I've seen it twice," Ollie said, "but I still want to see it again."

We got at the end of the line behind fifty gabbing, gangly junior high students and I wondered if I'd ever been hyperactive like that. They didn't talk, they yelled; they didn't laugh, they brayed; they couldn't just move their legs when they walked; their whole bodies got into the act—arms swinging, torsos swiveling, elbows out at right angles to their sides, their heads rotating around on their shoulders. There was something sort of awesome about being in the presence of so much energy.

"George!"

I knew the voice but couldn't quite place it, and

turned around. There stood Shirley King with her daughter.

"Don't tell me!" Shirl said.

I grinned. "Ollie's recommendation," I said. "Shirl, this is my brother Ollie; Ollie, this is Mrs. King from the Green Thumb, and her daughter Heather."

"Skip the 'Mrs. King' bit," Shirley said. She put out her hand, her gold bracelets clanking, and Ollie shook it awkwardly, taking a step backward as he did so. Heather was cringing in the other direction.

"If this isn't a *coincidence!*" Shirl went on, eyes on Ollie. "Heather talked me into seeing it, too. Where do you guys like to sit? Not too far down in front, I hope."

Ollie didn't answer.

"We could go by the Chocolate House after," Shirl went on, "and treat these kids to a malted. I mean, Heather thinks a malted is that air-blown fluff you get at McDonald's. You haven't lived till you've had a malted from the Chocolate House."

"Well . . ." I looked at Ollie. "What do you say?"

What *was* there to say? I realized too late that I should have announced a previous commitment. Said we had to go right home—do something. I imagined us sitting there in the Chocolate House for an hour while Shirl chattered on. "Maybe for a few minutes," I told her.

"Anybody who can't drink a malted in a few minutes, something's wrong with him," Shirl said. The line moved forward, we bought our tickets, and found ourselves in the center row of the theater. As Shirl edged into the row, she grabbed my hand and said, "Let's let them sit together—

get acquainted." It took me off guard and, like a jerk, I followed her toward our seats. Heather trailed after me, head down, then Ollie. Ollie sat with his eyes straight ahead, his body leaning to the right like the Tower of Pisa.

"He's so cute," Shirl whispered to me, her lips brushed my ear. "Aren't they darling together?"

I faked a weak smile. When the lights dimmed and the movie began, I felt like a heel. This was to be Ollie's Sunday. Wild horses couldn't have dragged him here if he'd known he had to sit with a ten-year-old girl he'd never met. She obviously felt the same way because she sat with both arms pulled in close to her body.

The movie started with a nighttime view of an African jungle, and the kind of music that sounds like footsteps following you down a dark alley. You moved along with the camera, down a narrow jungle path, leaves crowding in on either side of you, a snake slithering off to the left, and just as the music reached a crescendo, you saw, straight ahead, a huge, oddly shaped hill of earth, like an Indian burial ground, almost, with holes, maybe tunnels, in it, here and there. Nothing moved. The moon came out full. Then suddenly, the scene shifted, it was morning, and you were in the company of some UN anthropologists, who were trying to find out why the little wooden houses of the natives were disappearing with all the people in them. Shirl was leaning on my armrest, her hair almost in my eyes.

Another thing about junior high kids, I discovered, was that they talked all through the movie. Everybody, like Ollie, seemed to have seen the movie before, and they'd tell each other what to watch for next. Junior high kids have big mouths and small bladders, too. They were constantly popping up and down to go buy more candy or sodas, and five minutes later were off again to the restroom. It was like watching a movie through a picket fence; there were always bodies obstructing part of the screen.

Halfway through the film, one of the anthropologists died, and the others buried her in a wooden coffin. The footsteps-in-the-alley music again. The camera focused on the big mound of earth which started to twitch, then ripple, and suddenly this sort of hand—half-human, half-insect—came crawling out of the dirt.

I glanced over at Ollie. I knew that if we'd been sitting together, he would have been grinning, telling me that this was the good part. Instead, he just sat with his eyes facing front, his expression flat, about as far away from Heather as he could get.

On the other side, Shirley grabbed my arm and buried her face against my shoulder. "I can't look!" she giggled. "Tell me when it's over."

When the lights came on at last and we all made our way to the aisle, I said, "You know, Ollie, I don't think we dare go have a malted. Mom said she was serving dinner early. We'd better get home."

Ollie just looked at me.

"Oh, darn!" said Shirley. "Well, how about a raincheck! We'll do it another night. We've got a date at the Chocolate House now, the four of us."

When Ollie and I were in my car, I said, "I'm sorry, Ollie. Shirl's my boss—one of them, anyway

—at the Green Thumb. She just took me by surprise."

"Heather stinks," said Ollie.

"Oh, she was probably just as uncomfortable as you were," I told him.

"No, I mean she smells! Smells like her mother dumped a load of perfume on her. And I'm not going to the Chocolate House with them some other time, either. Not now or ever."

"I gotcha. I promise." I steered the car in the direction of the parkway. "Okay now, where do you want to go? I told Mom I was taking you out for dinner. You want pizza? Or should we go to Burger King? What'll it be?"

"Burger King," Ollie mumbled. By the time we turned off the parkway, though, he was beginning to come around. "What did you think was the best part, George? When the termite people broke into the coffin and began dismembering the corpse?"

I tried to keep a straight face. "Well, that was pretty good, but I liked the two termites fighting over the woman's brains, and the way her eye sort of fell out one side of her head and rolled down into a gulley."

"Oh, yeah! I knew you'd like that!" Ollie said.

I don't know how he managed to eat a bacon-burger after that. I sipped gingerly at a 7-Up and poked at a bag of fries while Ollie chattered on about a sequel.

They say that sometimes revelations come when you least expect them, and I never would have thought that one would come to me sitting there at Burger King. But I was thinking about the agony Ollie and Heather had gone through back there at the theater, thrown together that way. Thought about the struggles Heather must be having at home with a Mom who thinks she's perfect, and Ollie's struggle with parents who think he's anything *but*. Thought about all those noisy kids standing in line, and all the surprises and disappointments they're in for when they get to high school. And then, just as though I'd known it all the time, I knew what I wanted to be—what I wanted to do with my life. It was probably so far down the income scale that if it had been listed in the *Wall Street Journal* it would have been off the bottom of the page, about as far away from brain surgeon and lawyer as you could get. But it seemed so right for me that when I thought about it, my whole body was in agreement. I wanted to be a counselor in a junior high school. Mom and Dad would freak out.

There's a triangular patch of parkland across the street from the Green Thumb Garden Center, and some days I took my lunch over there to eat. Now and then a tall skinny guy who worked for a messenger service would buy a hot dog from the vendor and sit on a bench to eat it, waiting for his beeper to go off. Then he'd pick up his bike, walk to the pay phone across the street, and get his next assignment. Fred was his name. He'd balance his crash helmet on his knee while he ate, and sometimes we'd talk. I liked him, mostly, I guess, because he was about the only guy I knew who wasn't going to college in the fall. Fred was saving up to take a trip to South America on a freighter. That was another thing I liked about him. Guts.

He saw me eyeing his bike once, an old yellow Schwinn.

"Yeah," he laughed, "it's a trash bike. Some of the couriers ride those sleek European jobs that go the speed of light. But those are the bikes that get stolen. This old thing does the job—it'll travel when it has to."

"How much can you make in a week?" I asked him.

"Two-hundred, more or less. We get fifty per-cent commission. Another month or two, I figure, and I'll have saved enough to buy my ticket. Just in time to get on the boat before the cold weather gets here."

I was curious. "How *do* you get around when it snows?"

Fred just laughed and pointed to his feet. "Sometimes, between my feet and my bike, we're the *only* things moving in a snowstorm."

Employees at the Green Thumb only get a half hour off for lunch, there being so few of us. I'd just come back from lunch with Fred one day when Mr. Fletcher gave me a delivery.

"We've got some rose bushes to deliver to St. Sebastian's," he said. "I put four of them at the back of the greenhouse. You're to get there be-tween two and three, and someone will show you where to put them."

The bushes, set in redwood tubs, were huge. Harvey helped me get them in the van, and I was hoping I could take him along to deliver them, but Fletcher needed him to unload our first shipment of mums. I drove to St. Sebastian's, passing Fred on the way, his back bent, feet going like crazy. I tooted, and he waved.

I was able to pull up in the circular drive and park right outside the church. Someone had already propped the doors open. I pulled out the first tub, encircled it with my arms, and started up the steps. *Chablis, Hybrid White,* said a ticket tied to a bush; it blocked the vision in one eye.

Leaning against the rail to steady myself as I went up, I realized I should have gone inside first and found out where the heck I was taking the bush before I brought it in.

"Oh, good!" I heard someone say. "The flowers are here."

This is a tree, lady! I thought: *A whole, damn tree!* I staggered as I started down the center aisle.

"Right down there next to the altar," a voice said again, a different voice this time. I tried to see through the leaves, tried to connect this second voice with a face. I stopped and felt around with my foot till it hit something hard. Then slowly I bent my knees, and set the huge bush on the carpet. "Why . . . it's George Richards!" the voice said again. I stood up and turned around. There was Karen Gunderson, watching me in amusement.

"Karen!" I croaked, and then fell dumb.

"I didn't know you worked for the Green Thumb," she said. She was taller than I remembered, slim and utterly gorgeous in a pale blue blouse and skirt. She reached out and gently fingered one of the large white roses. "These are beautiful," she said. "Mother wanted live bushes

128

instead of cut flowers so she could start a rose garden in our yard, sort of a remembrance of my wedding."

I suddenly made the connection. "When's the big day?"

"Tomorrow." She smiled.

"Wow! The best of everything, Karen," I told her.

"Thanks," she said, as Bob Ellis waved from the side where he was talking with the minister.

I realized suddenly that I was not one of the wedding party, I was the delivery boy. I excused myself and went back out for the second bush.

"Two on each side," Karen's mother instructed, "the tallest toward the center."

By the time I staggered in with the last rosebush, they were rehearsing the ceremony. I moved awkwardly down a side aisle, pausing every so often to lean against a pew, then went a few paces more.

". . . for richer, for poorer, in sickness and in health . . ." the minister intoned. He stopped for a question from Karen, then went on again: ". . . forsaking all others, as long as you both shall live. . . ."

No! I wanted to yell. Don't do it, Karen, not till you've dated me! I held fast to the rosebush and clenched my jaw. I was remembering back to when I was ten, sitting in church between my folks, listening to the minister drone on and on. I used to get this horrible feeling that I might suddenly leap to my feet, yell, and turn handsprings down the aisle to the altar. I would imagine the shocked look on the minister's face, the way heads would turn, eyebrows raise, lips whisper. I'd imagine my mother's embarrassed gasp, and my dad coming down the aisle after me, carting me away. The more quiet and solemn the service, the more I distrusted myself, and I used to grip the edge of the seat to keep myself in check.

I set the last rosebush down on the rug near the altar and rearranged the leaves and branches. Then I took one last look at Karen. She had eyes only for Bob Ellis. I didn't yell, didn't beg, didn't turn handsprings down the aisle in protest. I went back outside, got in the van marked Green Thumb Garden Center, and drove away. And the following morning, according to the newspaper, Karen became Mrs. Robert Ellis and was on her way to a honeymoon in Jamaica.

The night before Bud Irving was to leave for college, his parents gave a little dinner for him at the Calhoun Beach Club. Discount invited the three of us—Dave, Psycho, and me—and we all arrived in coats and ties, four young men out to conquer the world.

We sat at the table making small talk with Mr. Irving because we couldn't begin to discuss his job with him, which was investment counseling. Mrs. Irving, her lavender dress matching the lavender tint in her hair, turned her martini around and around on the table and reminded us how long we'd all known each other, and that took a good fifteen minutes to sort out—who had known whom since first grade, at what point Dave moved into the neighborhood, and when it was that Psycho had transferred over from a parochial school. We joked and kidded a lot, ordering only those things on the menu we'd never heard of before and trying to figure out what they were once they got to the table. Underneath all the laughter, however, was the realization that things were changing, that the four of us were scattering to the winds. Even though we talked about what all we were going to do when we got together again at Thanksgiving, we wondered if we'd be the same, if things would ever again be the same as they were now.

We ended the meal with Crème Glacé, and Bud told his parents that we were going on down to the lake. We thanked Mr. and Mrs. Irving, shook hands all around, and said yes, how nice it was to be out of high school, getting out into the big wide world. Then the Irvings got in their Cadillac and the rest of us traipsed out to the parking lot to Bud's car.

"Hey, Discount, we can walk it," I said, but he only laughed at me.

"Listen, Gopher, the evening's not even started yet," he told me, and got a large bottle of vodka from his trunk.

Dave whistled. "Man," he said. "*We* are going to *party!*"

We carried the sack across the parking lot, across Lake Drive, and on down to the water.

There were three boats docked side by side along the wharf, and we figured the owners were having dinner back at the club. The deck lamps gave off just enough light that we could see the deck chairs and down into the cabins. We sat on the grass, backs against a tree, and passed the bottle around.

It should have been a fun evening, I guess, but

I had the strange and lonely feeling that I didn't belong. I could tell from the way the Irvings had steered the conversation away from college back there at dinner, that they thought it might hurt my feelings. Even the guys kept away from the topic, downplaying the packing, the decision of whether or not to take their stereos, the reputations of the girls on campus.

What was I accomplishing, anyway? I wondered. Ollie was signed up for eighth-grade algebra and was careening toward college, ready or not. I knew I wasn't going to work at the Green Thumb the rest of my life. How long, then? And why? How long does it take to make a statement?

Dave Hahn was the first one to sound drunk. He's got a slighter build, and alcohol gets to him sooner. He began that wheezing laugh he gets when he's drinking, and I thought, here we go again: rabbits. But Dave didn't want to talk rabbits this time; he wanted to talk about girls. While the boats bobbed up and down there by the wharf, Dave told us what he and his date had done on prom night in the stateroom of Wally Baisinger's cabin cruiser.

I'd already heard it, but not in such detail. Psycho hadn't heard it at all, and sat motionless, his lips slightly parted.

"Jeez, Dave, rack it up," I said, embarrassed. "I don't want to know every little move." I lied, of course.

Dave took off his jacket and spread it on the grass, then lay down. "But it was this gorgeous little mole—strawberry red—right on the edge of her tit," he said.

Psycho gave a little moan and reached for the vodka again. He slugged some more down.

"You know what?" said Bud, and his voice was a little too loud. "Know what? I heard that girls have a saying . . ." Bud sprawled out on his stomach. "Girls," he said again, his words slightly slurred, "have this saying, that if they don't get laid by prom night, they'll have seven years bad luck."

"Bullshit," I said. "That's a lot of bullshit, Discount. You made that up."

Bud raised up on one hand. "Honest! That's what my date told me. That's exactly what she said."

Dave was laughing again. "So did you put it to her, Discount? You save her from seven years bad luck?"

"Why not?" Discount said, and I knew he was lying. He'd told me the day after the prom that they hadn't gone that far. We were really full of it—all of us.

Only Psycho was silent. Every time the bottle went around, he took three slugs instead of two. I'm not the outsider, I remember thinking. Psycho's the outsider. Marsh hasn't even been out with a girl. Girls haven't been born, as far as he's concerned.

It made me feel better. We were still a team— Dave, Discount, and I. It was Psycho who didn't fit in.

"Hey, Marsh," I said, peering at him from around the tree trunk where we were sitting. "When you going to lay a girl?"

"Oh, shut up," said Psycho, glaring at me.

But the other guys picked it right up.

"Psycho's going to marry his cousin," Bud said, and we all whooped.

"How about *you?*" Marsh said to me. "How about you, Big Mouth? What'd *you* do on prom night? *You* score?"

I'd never talked too much with Marsh about my dates, never wanted him to feel bad—to feel left out. I'd certainly never told him how far I'd gone with Maureen. But this time it was different.

I grinned crazily at the others. "Let's just say that the next morning I had mosquito bites on my butt," I said, and Dave and Discount stared at me wide-eyed, then cheered.

"Way to go, Gopher!" Dave said. "How 'bout that?"

Marsh handed the bottle over to Discount and tried to stand up, but it took him two tries. We laughed. He sort of toddled down toward the water.

"Hey, Psycho, going to take a bath?" Dave yelled.

"He's got the hots from all this talk. Going to cool off," I said.

"Fuck off," Marsh said in answer. He grabbed hold of a post on the dock and stood there for some time, his back to us, his head bobbing slightly against the night sky as the water ebbed and flowed. We grinned at each other and finished off the bottle.

Marsh let go of the post finally and walked along the wharf. Then he jumped down onto the deck of the first boat, tied a few feet away.

"Psycho, get your ass out of there. They're likely to come back any minute," I yelled.

Marsh made no reply. We sat up and watched him. He was peering through the glass doors into the cabin. We laughed some more, and Psycho clowned around.

He climbed up on the bridge next and, leaning to one side, his hand against the cabin, made his way around the boat. When he had come full circle, he stood up on the edge of the deck, and with a loud "hi-yahhh!" leaped across three feet of water and onto the deck of the second boat.

We were cracking up, and Marsh seemed to enjoy the attention. He could be crazy too, he seemed to be saying. He too, could be a little wild. From where we sat, we could see him exploring the second boat, going up the ladder to the captain's chair at the very top, sitting awhile, then coming back down to peek in the cabin windows.

"Wouldn't it be a riot if there was some woman in there naked and she saw Marsh looking at her?" Bud said, and we were off again, almost sick with laughter. When you're drunk, you laugh at anything. The boat bobbed gently up and down, and we thought of all that vodka in Psycho's stomach. We laughed some more.

"He is going to be one sick dude," Bud observed. "I hope he doesn't heave on their deck chairs."

I was keeping one eye on the path leading up to the Beach Club. "Maybe we'd better go," I said.

"Who's going to drive?" Bud asked.

"We could just walk around awhile," I suggested. We got up and shook the grass off our coats. "Psycho!" I yelled. "Come on, now—we're going to walk around the lake."

Marsh only gave a whoop and went sailing through the air toward the third boat. One foot didn't quite make it, and we heard it scrabbling against the side of the boat as he tumbled onto the deck.

"C'mon, Marsh," I called again. "We're going to walk off the vodka."

Psycho only climbed up on the deck bench and with another "hi-yahhh!" leaped across the deck to the opposite bench. He teetered for a moment, then jumped down and began checking out the windows of the third cabin.

"Someone's coming, Psycho," Dave fibbed.

"We're going, Marsh," I called. We slung our jackets over our shoulders and walked a little way up the path.

"Hi-yahhh!" came Psycho's voice again. We saw him poised against the sky as he made the leap over to the second boat again, but this time it was followed by silence, then a splash.

"Jesus!" said Discount.

"Psycho?" I yelled.

Dave gave a short laugh. We waited.

"Marsh!" I yelled again, and started down to the water.

Suddenly Bud was running past me, kicking off his shoes, unbuckling his belt. I saw his pants drop, saw his body hit the water. None of us should have been in the lake.

I grabbed hold of the post and lowered myself down onto the first boat, then crawled over into the second, blinking my eyes, trying to clear my head. There was furious splashing, and Bud emerged between the second and third boats, his eyes huge and frightened.

"Is he down there?" I asked.

Bud didn't answer, just ducked under again.

"Is he there?" Dave yelled from the wharf. "Should I go for help?"

I peered over into the water. It was dark as chocolate pudding. I could hear it, but I couldn't see it. Bud came up again, and his mouth sagged as though he were crying. He dived down a third time.

"*Call* somebody!" I yelled to Dave. Then I stripped off my pants and went over the side.

TWELVE

I don't know which of us found him first. I re-member thinking that maybe he'd hit his head when he went over, and was lodged under one of the boats. The cold of the water almost forced the breath from me. I was moving hand over hand along the underside of the second boat when I ran into a tangle of arms and legs. Then both Bud and I were clawing our way to the surface, gasp-ing for air, pushing Psycho up over the side of the middle boat. Even before I could climb in myself, Bud was there on the deck, kicking deck chairs out of the way, stretching Marsh out flat on his back. I remember wondering if Discount was sober enough to be doing all this, but he was.

I kept telling myself that everything would be all right, because Bud was a trained lifeguard. I wiped the water out of my eyes, shivering there in my briefs, crawling over toward Bud, watching as he leaned over Psycho, tipping his head back, pinching his nostrils shut, listening for breath, his ear at Marshall's mouth.

Then his own mouth was over Psycho's, and I heard four quick breaths and watched as Mar-shall's chest rose. Bud reared back on his heels, his hair spewing droplets of water, and searched out the carotid artery on the side of Marshall's neck with his fingers.

"I got a pulse," Bud said, and then he said it again louder, as if to reassure himself. His voice was shaky.

"He's going to be all right then, isn't he?" I asked, but Bud was bending over again, pinching Psycho's nostrils, blowing into his mouth.

"*One* one-thousand, *two* one-thousand . . ." Bud counted aloud as he sat up, and when he reached *five* his head bobbed down again. He blew once more, and continued counting.

My own heart was pounding so violently that I could hear it—could feel the blood throbbing in my temples, each beat sending a rush of fear over me that was so intense it made me shiver. In the moonlight we watched Psycho's chest, waiting for the steady rise and fall that would signal he was breathing on his own.

Every five seconds, Discount leaned over Psycho again—another breath and another. His own face was contorted with terror.

"Oh, Christ! Breathe, Marsh, breathe!" he pleaded.

There were people on the path above us, looking down, talking to each other, wondering. Then the sound of footsteps as Dave came racing back.

"They're coming!" he yelled. "The rescue squad is on the way. Did you find him?" He jumped down into the first boat and looked over. "You *got* him!" he yelled. "Is he all right?"

"We've got a pulse," I told him, "but he's not breathing."

A crowd began to gather there on the wharf.

"Anything I can do?" a man called.

"An ambulance is coming," Dave told him, and climbed into the middle boat with us.

There was a gurgling sound, and suddenly a fountain of water and vomit came from Psycho's mouth. I wasn't sure what was happening, but Bud rolled him over on his side. Marsh was gagging, gasping. His hand moved. His head . . . Bud leaned over again, his arms around him.

We didn't say anything. All three of us were crying—sitting there on the deck surrounding Psycho, Bud and I without trousers, watching each other cry—and we didn't care.

The real fear—the sickening, head-twisting, gut-wrenching kind—didn't come until later, until I was home and lying on top of my bed, Typhus beside me, about as far from sleep as I could get, my clothes still clammy. Every so often another "what if" would wash over me, and I was drenched again in perspiration.

What if we hadn't found him in time? What if we'd been searching under the wrong boat? What if Marsh hadn't had any pulse either? What if he regained consciousness but was brain-damaged for life? I moaned aloud, paralyzed by possibilities. Typhus raised her head, whined, and tunneled back down against me.

By the time the rescue squad had arrived, Psycho had his eyes open and was talking. The boat's owner had arrived as well, wanting to know what the heck we were doing out there. Bud and I just pulled on our pants. Nobody answered him.

When the medics got Psycho back on the dock, though, he refused to go to the hospital. What was on all our minds, I think, was that we ought to get the heck out of there. At some point I saw Dave throw the vodka bottle far out on the lake. We didn't want to be there if a cameraman arrived—didn't want to make the newspapers the next day.

"You ought to be checked over," one of the men said to Psycho. "All that water in you. . . . Could be you did yourself some damage."

"No," Marsh told them, his voice hoarse. "I'm okay."

"You had a close shave there, buddy," another medic said, packing up his equipment. "This isn't any place to party."

I wondered how they knew.

An ambulance pulled up and then another, larger, rescue truck. Any minute KSTP would send a crew.

"We're taking him home," I told the medics.

They weren't all that happy about it.

"You eighteen?" they asked Marsh, and when he showed them his ID, they made him sign a release form. Slowly the crowd dispersed. The two ambulances up on Lake Street drove off, then the Rescue Squad.

We had known, however, that we couldn't go home. It was as though we were infectious, somehow. The terror would be contagious. One look at our faces, and our folks would crumble. And so we walked, Marsh leaning on us, and each of us with a hand on him somewhere—an arm around the shoulder, fingers gripping his arm. Around Lake Calhoun we went, Psycho with his clothes dripping.

"You're okay now, aren't you, Marsh?" we kept asking.

"God, you gave us a scare."

"Look, Psycho, we were all drunk, just shooting off our mouths. If anything had happened to you . . ."

"What'd I do?" Psycho asked. "Drink all the vodka?" He tried to make a joke of it.

Marsh, you bastard, I'd wanted to yell, we almost did you in. Just shut up, will you? But I didn't. We kept him walking and finally, around midnight, when we were sure he was okay, we drove to a Laundromat and put his pants and shirt in the dryer. Then, his clothes warm and strangely misshapen, we drove him home.

Along toward morning, I went down and sat on the back porch staring out over the lawn. I was thinking about Mr. and Mrs. Evans, asleep in their beds while their youngest son had been unconscious beneath a boat in Lake Calhoun. What his mom would have said, have done, if he'd drowned. It was me and my big mouth that had driven him down there—all because I was feeling low myself. Why? Because I wasn't going to college like the others. Why? Because, in a fit of rage, I'd said I wouldn't. Real mature.

The punishment handed out by your conscience, I discovered, was about a hundred times worse than any your parents could possibly impose on you. Again and again, like a videotape that wouldn't cut off, I saw Psycho lying in Saunders Funeral Home, saw me standing outside in my gray suit, directing parking, saw Dave and Discount and me as pallbearers, carrying Marsh out to the hearse.

I went back inside to wash up, but I didn't want to look at myself in the mirror. This was the guy who thought he could be a school counselor. Don't make me laugh.

The house was still. Mom and Dad slept on. The worst part of it all, strangely, was knowing that none of us would ever tell our parents. Something had happened that night that could have changed our lives, and theirs, forever—that maybe, in some ways, already had. As much as I wanted to talk about it, get it out, I couldn't do it—not with my parents—and I think the others felt the same way. It was something we would have to live with ourselves and, like a splinter under the skin, it hurt.

"Closest I ever came to drowning," said Shirl, "was when I was eight, and somebody pushed me into the deep end of the pool. Lifeguard didn't even see me."

In my need to tell someone, I had mentioned to Shirl that, over the weekend, I was horsing around down at the lake with some guys and one fell in.

"What happened?" I asked her.

"Some woman pulled me out. I'm draped over the edge of the pool on my stomach, gasping and gagging, and the lifeguard blows his whistle and tells me to get down to the shallow end." Shirl yanked a yellow leaf off a philodendron and dropped it in the large pocket of her apron. "That's the story of my life," she said dryly. "Nobody there when I need them, and when they *do* pay attention, it's for the wrong thing."

You had to keep a sharp ear tuned when Shirl talked in order to follow her exactly.

I seemed to have a need to tell everyone I could about the incident there at the lake, everyone who didn't know the Evanses, that is. All week I looked for reassurance that these things happen to everyone at some time or other. That we all have regrets. I was telling Fred, the courier, about how the real fear didn't hit me till later.

"I know what you mean," he said. "I was riding down Marquette last April when someone opened a car door on the driver's side. One minute the road was clear, and the next minute there was this glass and metal door before me, and then I was flying through the air. Like I was Superman or something." Fred took a large bite of his hot dog and chewed thoughtfully, teeth grinding noisily. "And all the while I was in the air—it couldn't have been more than a couple seconds—I was thinking, My God, I'm going to die. I tried to aim my body toward the grass beyond the curb, but I couldn't, of course. I was heading for concrete."

He stopped eating and pointed to a scar below his right ear. "I was lucky," he said. "But the thing is . . ." He took another bite. "The thing is, all the while I was in the air, it was like I was sitting back somewhere, watching myself—like I wasn't really there. When I hit, I was conscious of the pain, but not the possibility that someone might run over me. It was later, when I thought about it again—about all that *might* have happened— that I got the cold whammies."

I told Anne about it when we were watering the display of mums by the front entrance—how we'd had dinner with Bud's parents there at the club and then gone down to the lake.

"What was the occasion?" she asked at last.

"Just celebrating," I said. "The end of high school, I guess." The end of high school and the beginning of something else, I thought, only I wasn't sure what the something was.

Compared to Psycho's near-miss, nothing else seemed important. The following Sunday, for example, I woke about ten to the sound of voices in Jeri's room. She and Mom were obviously arguing. I didn't even know what it was about, but it seemed trivial, somehow.

Mom's voice first: "What is *that* supposed to mean?"

Then Jeri's voice, growing louder: "Just what I said, Mother. I'm careful. Do I have to spell it out?"

"Yes, you certainly do! If it's what I think . . ."

"Oh, no telling *what* you think!" Jeri retorted, and I heard her footsteps crossing the hall, then the slam of the bathroom door.

"Jeri!" Mother called, standing outside it. "If it means grounding you every single night of your junior year, I'm prepared to do that. You know that, don't you?"

There was no answer from the bathroom, but a few seconds later I could hear the splash of the shower.

I waited for five minutes, then got up, pulled on my jeans, and went down to the kitchen for some orange juice. When I reached the doorway, I saw Mom sitting at the table with her hands over her face, and when she heard me, she turned her head away and I saw her swallow. Behind me, Dad came in the front door with *The New York Times* and went on into the living room to read it. I slowly poured a glass of juice, watching Mom out of the corner of my eye. She seemed smaller than usual, dwarfed by the high collar of her robe, her arms swallowed up in the sleeves.

I'd planned to take the juice up to my room, but felt maybe I ought to say something.

"Problems?" I said finally, taking a sip.

Mom nodded, biting her lip, and swallowed again. "I guess you could say that."

I leaned against the refrigerator. Mom still had her face turned away as though she didn't want me to see that her eyes were red. Finally she said, "You know, the trouble with being a parent is that we're always so new at it." She ran one hand over her eyes and then turned her face in the other direction, toward the window. "I mean, by the time the last child is through his 'terrible twos,' and we've finally learned to cope, the terrible twos are over. Same with everything else. I thought that once Patricia was through her teens, I would know how to deal with a teenage girl. I don't. Jeri's so different. I discovered I'm still new at being a mother."

I set my glass on the counter. "Well, if it's any consolation, Mom, Jeri's still new at being sixteen. I guess we're all sort of playing it by ear."

Mom smiled ruefully and finally looked me in the eye. "What's that phrase you always say— 'life's weird'? Well, that's it, I guess." She pushed away from the table and got up to pour herself some more coffee. ". . . I'm not asking you to tell on your sister, and I'm not asking if you know anything I don't know about her. But I caught her coming in long after she should have been home last night, and I have the feeling this isn't the first time. If you have any advice—suggestions, whatever—I'd appreciate it."

Mom really caught me off guard. "If I think of anything," I told her, "I'll let you know."

"Thanks," she said. Mom stood over by the window drinking her coffee. "Life *is* weird," she said again. "Because you know what I decided last night while I was waiting for Jeri to come home? That, after all these years of going to night school for my master's, I'm going to refuse a promotion."

I stared. Was this *my* mother talking? "How come?"

"Because I don't want to leave the classroom. I like teaching, I hate administrative work, so why get a promotion just to do something I don't enjoy? It doesn't make sense." She put her cup back down, and I saw a relief on her face I hadn't seen for a long time, if not for Jeri, then for herself. "Life's too short to spend it doing something I don't like. I won't be out anything but a little extra money, which we don't need all that much, and my pride. And I guess I can do with a little less of that, too. Right?" She smiled at me. Grinned, actually.

I grinned back. "It'll be nice seeing you stick with something you really enjoy," I told her.

We were both leading with our chins. It was my chance to say that since she'd decided that for herself, couldn't she extend the same privilege to Ollie? And it was her chance to say it would be nice to see *me* doing something I really enjoyed, too, and did I really expect her to believe I wanted to spend the rest of my life hauling bushes around and bagging fertilizer? Neither of us, however, took that chance.

I realized, after I'd gone upstairs, that this was probably the most open, honest conversation Mom and I had had in a long time. On her part, anyway. We were both listening to each other for a change. In the past, it was as if we tuned the other out. Whose fault was that? For once I decided that no one had to take the blame. We were both new at being whatever we were.

When I went to work on Monday, there was another problem even more immediate than Jeri.

"Listen," Shirl said when I walked in, "I'm planning a little surprise birthday supper for Heather tonight; I'm taking her to the Lake Street Garage, and I'd like you and your little brother to join us. My treat."

The Lake Street Garage was Ollie's favorite hamburger place, with the cab of a 1942 Chevy truck parked among the tables, but I knew better than to get Ollie mixed up in that. And because I was so busy concocting an excuse for Ollie, I walked right into the trap myself—said that Ollie already had something planned, but I'd be glad to come.

"Good!" said Shirl. "Heather will love it."

As the morning wore on, it occurred to me that I probably ought to buy Heather a present. I told Anne about the invitation. "What do you give an eleven-year-old girl for her birthday?" I asked.

"Other eleven-year-old kids at the party," Anne said sardonically.

She was right, of course, but since that wasn't my responsibility, I walked over to the Sweet Shoppe on my lunch break and bought Heather a box of chocolate golf balls.

I saw Fred on my way back, walking his bike over to the phone booth on the corner.

"Two more weeks!" he called. "My bags are packed."

"I'll treat you to lunch on your last day," I yelled back.

It bothered me more than I let on that Fred was leaving. Minneapolis seemed a little too quiet somehow. I still went to Psycho's to weightlift, but sometimes he stayed on campus late to study, and I didn't like working out alone, especially in the Evanses' basement, especially after what had almost happened to Marsh. Everyone except me seemed to have plans. Fred had been working as a messenger for a year and a half to save up for his trip to South America. Anne was in school part-time, paying her own way as she went. It wasn't that I was working that bothered me so much; it was that I wasn't working for a reason.

It started raining about four that afternoon, and I got to the Lake Street Garage about six-thirty, dripping water from my hair. Shirl and her daughter were already in a booth waiting for me, Shirl on one side, Heather on the other next to a pile of raincoats and a wet umbrella. I slid in beside Shirl and handed Heather the cellophane box from the Sweet Shoppe.

"Happy birthday, Heather," I said.

She stared at the box. "What are they?" she asked, her arms pressed rigidly to her sides.

"Well, *take* it, sweetie, and find out!" Shirl urged, and then turned to me. "Now aren't you nice!"

Heather opened the box and peered down at the chocolates, then picked one up between her fingers.

"Chocolate golf balls!" Shirl said.

"Thank you," Heather told me, and dropped it back in the box.

"She'll have one for dessert," Shirl said.

While we were waiting for our order of hamburgers and fries, I remembered what Anne had said about eleven-year-old friends. At a table across from us, a Brownie troop slurped malteds, and in the booth behind us, a family with three kids made a joyful racket. Heather watched the Brownies blowing straws at each other across their table, giggling and diving down on the floor to pick up the paper wrappers.

When the food arrived, it gave us something to do. The fries were big and thick, cooked with the skins on. I'd eaten half of mine when I realized that Heather not only did not act like a kid, she didn't eat like one either; she took little nibbles like a thirty-year-old woman, her forearms resting politely on the table, napkin spread out in her lap.

Shirl did most of the talking—about how Heather was exactly the same size and weight as Shirl had been at that age, and how, when she got to high school, the boys were going to go mad over her.

"Sit up straight, honey," she told Heather. "Posture is the absolute key to a good figure."

I could have eaten two hamburgers without even trying, but Shirl was paying, and I slowed down halfway through my malted to give the appearance of being full. "Great food," I told her.

"It's Heather's favorite place," she answered. "We should do this more often—the three of us. Make it a tradition, like the first Monday of every month. Would you like that, sweetie?" she asked Heather. Her daughter didn't answer.

"Oh, God, it's hard to relax after working all day," Shirl said suddenly, shoving her plate away and leaning her elbows on the table. She tipped her head back and closed her eyes. "It's my neck where I feel it most. Always the neck. Massage it a little, would you, George?"

The words sort of marched along the edge of the table and stopped in front of me.

"Excuse me?" I said.

"My neck," said Shirl, pointing, her eyes still closed. "Get the kinks out for me."

I swallowed. I tried to think of some funny excuse, but my mind went blank. I raised my arm and put my hand tentatively on the back of Shirl's neck, giving a few feeble rubs.

"Oh, harder!" Shirl said, shoulders hunching. "Right above the shoulder blades. Oh, God, yes! Right there!" She shivered slightly.

Across the table, Heather watched without expression.

After ten seconds or so, I started to remove my hand, but Shirley reached up and grabbed it. "Don't stop, you've hardly started!" she said. "Oh, that's what I wanted. It feels so good!"

I could feel the heat in my own neck, my face, my ears. Across the aisle, one of the Brownies had spotted us. Her eyes narrowing in delight, she whispered to the girl beside her, who whispered, in turn, to the next girl. One by one gleeful faces turned in our direction, then ducked down in a spasm of giggles. Heather shifted uncomfortably.

I stood up suddenly. "Just remembered," I said. "I forgot to tell Mom I wouldn't be home for dinner. Excuse me."

"Hurry back," said Shirl.

I walked across the room to the pay phone in one corner and put a quarter in. I had only planned to fake it, but in all the embarrassment, my sweaty hand dialed our number.

"Mom," I said, when she answered. "I'm down here at the Lake Street Garage having dinner with Shirley King and her daughter and I need an excuse to leave."

There was a pause at the other end. "I *wondered* where you were," she said, and I could tell that she was laughing. "How old's the daughter?"

"Eleven," I croaked.

Mom laughed out loud. "Well, Grandpa Richards is here for dinner, and you could always tell your boss that you forgot we were having company, which is the actual truth of the matter."

"Thanks," I said gratefully. "I'll fill you in later."

I strode quickly back to the table. "Boy, did I ever goof!" I said. "We've got company for dinner, and I was supposed to be home a half hour ago."

"Oh, George! What a shame!" Shirl said. "What are you going to do? You just ate!"

"Wing it, I guess. Maybe I can stuff down a few bites of chicken or something."

"Well, thanks for coming. Wasn't it nice that he could be here for your birthday, Heather?"

"Thank you very much," Heather said.

"You're welcome," I told her, and leaned down over the table. "And next year, when you're twelve, I hope your mom brings you back here again with a whole carload of friends, and you're the noisiest table in the room."

Heather looked at me with her large brown eyes, and for just a moment I thought I saw a glimmer of feeling in them. She gave me a faint smile.

Shirl grabbed my hand and squeezed it. "Thanks, George," she said. "See you tomorrow."

When I got outside, I walked a block in the rain before I remembered to put on my jacket. I held it over my head and made a run for my car. It was as though I were running for my life somehow. I wondered what the heck I was going to do.

THIRTEEN

As I was passing Dad's study Wednesday night, he called me in.

"Got a minute?" he asked.

I came in and leaned against the door, waiting. Dad was fiddling around with some papers on his desk.

"When we had that . . . talk last spring," he said without looking up, "I told you I'd pay for your food, shelter, and medical expenses, and you've been contributing some of your own earnings every week." He stopped. "Which we appreciate," he added brusquely. "Since you've proven yourself responsible, I think it's only fair to offer you the interest on the thousand dollars I'd put away for your spending money—books and things—during your freshman year of college. The principal, of course, stays in the bank, but the interest comes to about twenty-five dollars a quarter. If you'd like it, I'll write a check."

Why did I get the feeling that he still wanted to call the shots—wanted me to feel that I was being rewarded for doing something he wanted me to do, not for anything I did on my own initiative?

My first impulse was to say, "You can keep your

precious money, Dad. I can get along without it."
But then I realized that—clumsy as it was—it
was a peace offering on his part.

"Sure," I said. "That'd be fine."

Dad got out his checkbook and picked up his
pen.

As I put the check away in my drawer afterwards, I was thinking about how I really did want
to be friends with him again—the way we used
to be, I mean—watching David Letterman together, making chocolate sodas at night with Dad's
seltzer water. It couldn't just be on his terms,
though, but maybe it didn't have to be. Maybe he
was willing to bend a little. I wondered if Mom's
decision not to take a promotion had any impact
on him, if they both weren't beginning to see that
the only career worth devoting your life to was
one that you enjoyed. Dad had even said as much
himself: figure out what you like to do best and
see what you come up with, he'd suggested. It
was just that he didn't seem to think much of
what I liked best, kept thinking maybe he could
change that.

I got a second present on Friday. Just as I was
putting the shovel away in the greenhouse, ready
to go home, Shirl called me over the intercom and
asked me to come to the office.

"For you," she said, and handed me a box
wrapped in blue and purple paper, tied with a
blue ribbon.

"What's this?"

"For your birthday," she said. "Your belated
birthday. I looked you up in the files and saw that
you were eighteen in July; I didn't so much as
wish you happy birthday."

I was embarrassed. "Jeez, Shirley, you and Fletcher make a habit of celebrating the employees' birthdays?"

"It's not from Mr. Fletcher, it's from me, and you're not just *any* employee," she said, which is what I was afraid of. "Open it," she said, her lips next to my ear.

I glanced around uncomfortably. I could see Anne already heading out the door toward her car, heard Fletcher's truck rumbling up the road past the greenhouse, and Harvey talking to himself in the stockroom. I unwrapped the box, wondering what I should do. Whatever it was, should I give it back? Tell her I couldn't accept it?

I was looking down at a dress shirt with narrow blue and white stripes, and the monogrammed letters, GTR, on the pocket.

"How did you know my middle initial?" I asked. I felt as though Shirley King had invaded my room somehow, my privacy, my life.

She laughed. "It's there on your application. Don't be so surprised."

"Well . . . man, it's really nice!" I said. Then I realized I *had* to accept it. You don't return a shirt with initials on the pocket. "You really shouldn't have done it, though. I don't know how Mr. Fletcher would feel about it."

This time there was a trace of annoyance in Shirl's voice. "What does Fletcher have to do with it?" she snapped. "This is a personal present from a friend to a friend. Okay? Did you have to ask Fletcher if you could give Heather a gift? Now, if you don't *like* it . . . !"

"Shirl, it's beautiful. Really. I just wasn't expecting it."

Her face went soft then. "I want to see you wear it sometime."

"Sure." I laughed. "Next time I load the truck."

I felt numb when I went to work the next Monday, but it wasn't from the cold. I could see my breath in the air when I went outside and there was even a half inch of snow on the ground. But I liked slipping into my sheepskin-lined jacket, my heavy gloves, and walking up the hill with Mr. Fletcher to put a load of saplings on the truck. I considered asking him if I could work outside only, but that meant he'd have to hire someone else to help out in the shop. He'd made it clear when he took me on that I was to fill in wherever I was needed.

"I like working outside best," I told him.

"Who doesn't?" He laughed, helping me drag a huge bag of pine chips off the truck. "Me, I grew up on a farm. You can take the boy out of the country, they say, but you can't take the country out of the boy. I had my way, we wouldn't even have a shop—all them googaws. But we get an awful lot of folks who come in to buy something in the shop and end up out here looking over the evergreens, so I got to keep it going." He wiped his hands and looked around. "After we unload those pumpkins over there, I want you to give Shirl a hand—put some pumpkins in the window of the shop. That always brings in a crowd around Halloween."

This time it wasn't so bad because Anne came in about one, and she and Shirley and I all set to work carving jack-o'-lanterns to put in the window. I gave mine a sardonic smile, one eyebrow up, the other down. Anne's was definitely the most creative, though, with corn husks for hair, an apple for the nose, pine cone ears, and acorn eyes. But Shirl said that mine was the winner, hands down. I didn't even know it was a contest.

"Listen," I said, walking out to the parking lot with Anne after work. "Would you like to see a movie Saturday night? There's a Hitchcock revival on at the Uptown."

"That sounds like fun," said Anne. "What time?"

My heart leaped, just as though this were my first date or something. "I'll let you know later," I said, and she gave me her number.

On Wednesday, Shirl called me back in the stockroom to help get some planters down from a high shelf, and just when I was on the next to the top step of the ladder and had both arms in the air, she said, "Guess what, George? Heather's Dad is coming to town this weekend and he's going to take her for a few days."

"That'll be nice for Heather," I said, and slowly slid one of the heavy planters forward so that I had it secure in both hands.

"Nice for Heather, maybe, but not for me. If there's one thing I can't stand, it's an empty apartment."

The planter suddenly seemed twenty pounds heavier in my hands.

"You could always ask in some girlfriends to play cards," I said, and slowly, carefully, moved my left foot down to the next step on the ladder.

"Now *that* is about the most boring suggestion I ever heard," she said. "I didn't think you were capable of anything quite so deadly."

"Sorry," I said.

I could feel her hand on my leg, steadying me as I descended the ladder.

"Actually," she said, "I was thinking about you. Why don't you come over on Saturday night? Bring some records. I want to hear what young men are listening to these days. Surprise me."

Terror and relief went zigzagging through my body. "Gee, I'm sorry, Shirl, but I've already made plans for Saturday night."

Her voice turned into a little-girl whine. "I should have known," she said. "A girlfriend, I'll bet." And then, so quickly I couldn't answer, "No, don't tell me. Just come over Sunday night instead. Heather's not coming home till Monday morning."

"Well, I don't know . . ." I told her.

She laughed. "That's an order, soldier. I'm your superior officer, remember? What do you like to eat? I'll make the dinner myself."

"I don't know," I said again. "Look, I'll let you know later, okay?"

I fled the room. The shop, in fact. It was a quarter of twelve and we could eat whenever we liked. Usually, when it was cold out, I ate my sandwich there in the stockroom, but this time I grabbed the paper sack, threw on my jacket, and went over to the park. The benches were all empty, of course. Even the hot dog vender was gone. My teeth chattered.

I'd never been in a situation like that before. Even if I got out of going to Shirley's apartment that weekend, she'd only ask me again. I was already in up to my ears. The one thing I knew I couldn't do was tell Fletcher what his Girl Friday was up to. No way.

I thrust my hands in my pockets and had just started back toward the Green Thumb when Fred came riding by on his Schwinn, a package under his arm, heading for the office building down the street.

"Fred!" I yelled, and sprinted across the park.

"I'm on a job," he yelled back.

"I don't care! Wait!" I ran over and grabbed his handlebars as he swerved to a stop.

"What's the matter?" he said, looking at me strangely.

"When are you quitting?" I asked him.

"Friday's my last day. I'll fly to San Francisco and take the boat on Monday."

"I want your job," I told him.

He stared at me. "What?"

"I want your job. Tell me how to apply, where to go."

"Well . . . sure! You just get fired or something?"

"No. I'm going to quit."

He kept looking at me. "You got a bike?"

"I'll buy yours."

Fred scratched his head. "You realize it's almost winter," he said. "It's going to be cold out here on the streets."

"It's going to be one heck of a lot colder back at the Green Thumb," I told him. "Meet me here Friday, and I'll write you a check, okay? I owe you lunch, remember? Your last day."

He took off, waving his helmet at me, and I went on back to the garden center.

I had an opportunity to speak to Fletcher when I worked the greenhouse that afternoon.

"Mr. Fletcher," I said, when I was sure that we

were alone. "I'm sorry to have to tell you this, because you took a chance on me, but I'd like to leave this job as soon as you can find a replacement."

Fletcher was bending over, pulling at a bag of peat moss. Slowly he straightened. "How come? You going to college? Got another job?"

"Not yet."

"You don't like it here?" he questioned. "I don't pay enough?"

"I like the work, and the pay is fine," I said. I could feel my ears getting pink. "It's just . . . well, I'd really rather not say. You've been swell, and I'm sorry about this, that's all."

Fletcher's eyes seemed almost to change color, as though they had sucked up all the expression on his face. Finally he sighed, a big sigh, and bent over the peat moss again, dragging it over to a pile of sacks in the corner.

"Well, George . . . I think I understand, so you don't have to say any more." He stood up again and went on talking, standing sideways, his big hand rummaging about in a box of tulip bulbs. "Shirl—she means well, she really does, but she's lonely, and I know she don't get on with everybody. I'm not about to let her go, though. She's my second wife's niece, and she knows the shop inside and out." He turned his back on me then and began straightening a row of African violets, and I heard him mutter, as if to himself, "Gol-darn it, though, I'm going to have to hire me a hunch-backed, snaggle-toothed man with a peg leg for Shirl to leave him alone, I swear it." Then, "When you want to go?"

"As soon as you can let me."

"Work the week out," he said, "and I'll have your paycheck ready on Friday. And George . . ." He turned finally in my direction and put out his hand. "No hard feelings, either."

Shirley scarcely spoke to me for the rest of my time at the garden center. Nothing I did could please her, however. The concrete bowls for the birdbaths, which I had stacked a dozen times before, suddenly weren't stacked right any longer. The floor wasn't swept to her satisfaction. The shelves had not been dusted on schedule, and never mind that Fletcher had needed me in the greenhouse. I don't know what all he told her about my leaving, but Shirl was in a sour mood the rest of the week. I was afraid she'd find out I was dating Anne and make things rough for her, so I worked like a dog and didn't socialize with anybody.

I was embarrassed that I hadn't handled it better, Shirl's flirtation with me. It was a measure of my own awkwardness, I guess, that I couldn't think of anything to do but quit. It must happen to other people in other businesses, I thought. The mature person would probably have known exactly the right thing to say, firm yet polite and generous; something that would help Shirl save face. What would my dad have done if it had ever happened to him, I wondered?

On Friday, I met Fred at the park and there was a grin on his face so large he could hardly contain it. He showed me his ticket on the freighter, the *Dama de Acera,* and I wrote him out a check for his yellow Schwinn and bought him lunch.

"Here's the man to see on Monday," Fred told

me, handing me a slip of paper. "I told Benson you'd be in for an interview, so he's expecting you. He'll give you a rough time—it's just his way—but be sure to have a map of the city along. He might put you right to work."

"Good luck, Fred," I told him. "Your trip sounds great."

"It's something I've wanted to do my whole life, six months on a freighter," he said. "If I don't do it now, I might never do it."

When we'd finished eating, I wheeled the Schwinn back to my car and, by tipping one of the front seats forward, managed to wedge the bike behind. That seemed important, somehow, what Fred had said—about doing what he'd always wanted to do, so he might as well do it now. What was it *I* had always wanted to do? I was leaving the Garden Center to join the Minneapolis Messengers, from one kind of "go-for" job to another. The more I thought about what I wanted to do with my life, the more I felt I wanted to go into counseling. Maybe it was a way of straightening myself out, I don't know, but it appealed to me. The Minneapolis Messenger Service wasn't getting me one step closer to that, but I couldn't do much about it now.

I decided that when I left at the end of the day, I was going to go up to Shirl and tell her good bye whether she was speaking to me or not. I was going to say that I wished her the best of luck— her and Heather. Shirl made things easy for me, though. She wasn't there. She'd gone to lunch at noon and hadn't come back, and Anne said she'd told her she had a dental appointment. I was both sorry and relieved. I'd wanted to think I was big enough to carry it off. Shirl didn't give me that chance.

I told the folks at dinner that I'd quit. I didn't have to, but I knew they'd have questions later, and I wanted to head them off.

"It wasn't the work," I said. "I liked it fine. And it wasn't the boss. I just felt it was time to move on."

Dad continued mashing his potato and said, "Got something else in mind?"

"I'm going to see a man about a courier job on Monday," I told him.

Dad mashed a little more. "Well, let us know." End of conversation. Mom didn't say anything at all. No probing. No advice. Just three adults talking to each other. I *almost* wished they'd ask something else, but no use in their learning to let go if I was just going to hang on.

On Saturday I drove over to Edina to pick up Anne. She was wearing a bulky red sweater and jeans, with little gold earrings in her pierced ears. She looked great, and I told her so.

"Thanks," she said, settling down on the seat beside me. "And you look like a guy who's been relieved of a hundred-pound weight on his shoulders. Was the job getting to you all that much?"

"It wasn't the job," I said simply, and let it go.

The movie was *Rear Window*, which I'd seen but Anne hadn't; I would have sat through anything, even *Heidi*, to sit through it with Anne. She was easy to be with in a movie. I mean, she didn't whisper through it or make a racket with popcorn or anything. You can tell a lot about a girl just taking her to a movie. I took a girl once to see a comedy who laughed in all the wrong places.

"So that was Grace Kelly!" Anne said later as we walked back to my car. "I've heard Mom talk about her."

We drove to Bread and Chocolate and ordered cups of espresso along with a plateful of pastries to share—a cheese croissant, a sourdough roll, blueberry muffins, and a Suicide Fudge Bar.

"Heaven!" Anne said as she bit into the chocolate and rolled it around on her tongue.

The first time you take someone out, there are all sorts of things to talk about. All your old jokes are new, all your old stories exciting. So you know what we talked about, Anne and I? Ollie. I'd started by asking Anne what she was majoring in at the U, and she'd said she wasn't sure yet, that she was taking some ecology courses in a program called *Conservation and Resource Development*.

"I'm hoping that something will click, and I'll figure out what my major will be later," she told me. "That's why I'm taking it slow right now, going part-time, till I'm sure."

"Makes sense," I'd said.

"Maybe marine biology or zoology or something."

"A forest ranger, maybe?" I'd asked, thinking of Ollie.

"No, but they're all related."

Then I told her about my brother and his troubles with Spanish and the way my folks had him lined up for college.

"I'm sorry to say that if Ollie gets a B.A. in forestry, he'll probably have to take German," Anne said, "Goes way back to the old forest *meisters*—masters of the forest—something like that. But there are all sorts of jobs he could get in the field without a degree. I've got a boxful of pamphlets at home. I'll sort through them and see which ones might be right for Ollie. They'll tell him what courses to take, where to apply. . . ."

"Anne," I told her as we split the last croissant, "you might be the best thing that's ever happened to Ollie, you know it?" And then I added, "Or to me, too."

Anne just smiled.

When I drove her home, though, she said something else. She said that we had talked about Ollie's plans and her plans and that I'd even told her about my two sisters. What about me? she wanted to know. I was leaving the Green Thumb Garden Center and starting work with Minneapolis Messengers, but where was I headed? What was the game plan?

I didn't have an answer to that. I told her I was still sorting things out. The understatement of the year.

On Sunday, I really wanted to call Anne again, but I decided not to rush her. I went to Grandpa Richards' apartment instead. Whenever the Minnesota Vikings play the Chicago Bears, you know that Gramps is glued to the set. The game was scheduled for noon, and I stopped at the deli for the shrimp and pasta salad that he likes.

"Come on in," he called when I knocked. "Door's open." The game had already begun, and Gramps was parked about six feet from the set, a TV dinner on his lap.

"You want a TV dinner, put one in," he said, scarcely taking his eyes off the game for a moment.

I set the container of shrimp on his tray and saw him smile. "Go get yourself a fork," he said.

We never talk until the commercials. Gramps has to hear every word the announcers say, so when the Bud Lite commercial came on, Gramps said, "How's the job?"

"I quit," I said, and speared a shrimp.

"*Quit?*" It was as though the word itself left a bad taste in his mouth. I'd forgotten; the Richardses never quit. "What's the matter? Work too hard for you?" he asked.

There was more than a touch of sarcasm in his voice, but I decided to ignore it.

"There was a woman boss putting the moves on me; it freaked me out," I told him, then realized I had to translate. "She was giving me presents and asking me over, and I just couldn't handle it."

Gramps' fork paused in midair, then slowly continued the journey to his mouth and a tortellini disappeared. "She was the boss, huh? Nobody over her?"

"Mr. Fletcher, but I think he already knew. I think it's happened before. He said he didn't want to lose her, and I didn't think it was right to tell him everything."

"No, probably not. Wouldn't have been the gentlemanly thing to do," said Gramps.

The commercials were over, and when the game began again, the Bears fumbled the ball.

"Hot *dog!*" Gramps always says on a fumble, an interception, or a touchdown. I got so interested in the game I forgot what we'd been talking about, but the next time a commercial came on, Gramps said, speaking of Fletcher, "Well, that's a heck of a way to run a business. What are you going to do?"

"I think I've got a messenger job lined up. Going to see the man tomorrow."

"What sort of messenger?"

"A bicycle courier."

"You got a bike?"

"I bought a used one."

Gramps reached out for the remote control and muted the sound. "I've got to hand it to you, George," he said. "You always land on your feet." He sat thinking for a minute, then added, "There's something to be said for being your own man. Wish someone had said that to me when I was eighteen."

I studied Gramps there, clutching the remote control as though it were important he have control over something. "You wouldn't have gone to law school?" I asked tentatively.

"Probably would have, but it would have been because *I* wanted to go. There's a difference." The game came on again; Gramps pressed the button, releasing the sound, and it was almost as though our conversation had never been.

And yet it had. I remembered what Gramps had said at Christmas, about how you could be "right", but for the wrong reasons. Dad and Mom were "right," in a way, that I belonged in college; it's just that some of the *reasons* they had for wanting me there were a little suspect. Partly they wanted me to go to college for myself, but partly for them, too. I wanted to talk to Gramps some more about it, but he was intent on the game, and during the next break, he didn't bring the subject up again.

"There's half a Sara Lee coconut cake in the refrigerator," is what he said. I started to tell him I didn't want any, then realized that he did, so I went out, cut him a slice and brought it back on a saucer.

It was about halfway through the second quarter that the Vikings, down by seven, intercepted the ball and made a touchdown, all the way down the field. I was on my feet yelling, waiting for the usual, "*Hot* dog," which was sometimes accompanied by the stamp of a foot, but this time Gramps didn't say anything at all.

"Did you *see* that?" I said. "From the twenty-yard line! Man, they are *hot!*"

I looked over at Gramps. The coconut cake sat untouched on his plate, and one arm dangled awkwardly at Gramps' side.

"Hey, Gramps!" I said, leaning over.

He turned and looked at me blankly; one side of his mouth sagged. His lips moved, but I couldn't hear what he said. I picked up the remote control and muted the sound.

"What?" I asked.

Gramps was drooling just a little, and then he spoke again, but it was absolute nonsense. The syllables weren't even words.

"Are you all right?" I said.

I picked up his fork and handed it to him, shoving the cake a little closer. But his arm continued to dangle there at his side. He looked at the fork and then at me, and then I saw the fear in his eyes. Something was wrong, and Gramps knew it.

I went to the phone and dialed home.

FOURTEEN

We found out that Gramps had had another stroke—his second. The first one, a year ago, had hardly affected him at all. But this one was different.

It's pretty scary to talk to a graduate of Harvard Law School and have him answer you in gibberish. To lift him from his chair and discover that his right arm and leg are useless. It was a good sign, though, the doctor said, that Gramps was conscious, but the next few days would tell us a lot about how fully he would recover. As soon as we got the diagnosis, Dad called his sister in Duluth, and Aunt Sylvia said she'd fly down that evening and take over in Gramps' apartment.

I spent the next few hours driving back and forth between Gramps' place and the hospital, bringing him things that Mom thought he might need. Then I picked up Aunt Sylvia at the airport and helped Dad look through Gramps' desk to see if any bills were due or if he had any appointments that needed cancelling. It was almost midnight by the time we finally got to bed.

The alarm went off at six-thirty the next morning, an hour earlier than usual. Fred had told me

I should be waiting there at the Minneapolis Messenger Service when they opened, with a map of the city, my bike, the crash helmet I'd bought from him, and some kind of rain gear. In other words, ready to work.

I didn't shower, because Fred said it didn't make any sense to do it before work. The thermometer read in the low forties, so I put on sweatpants over my gym shorts, a sweatshirt over my T-shirt, and black high-top sneakers over heavy socks. I ate the breakfast Fred had recommended—two peanut butter and jelly sandwiches with a glass of milk—and was waiting outside the MMS office at seven fifty-three.

A woman was the first to arrive. She eyed me warily and said I could come in and wait for the dispatcher, Hal Benson. Her job was lining up new clients, she said, and made it perfectly clear that she had nothing whatever to do with the sweaty part of the business.

Hal Benson got there at one minute before eight, a small man with a large stomach. He was not impressed with my being there on time, not impressed with the map I'd brought, or with anything else about me. He was letting me work that day, he said, because he hadn't found a replacement yet for Fred. He gave me a beeper, asked if I had enough change to call the office when necessary, and after I'd filled out an employment form, he sent me on my first job: I was to pick up a set of blueprints from an office on Eighth Street and deliver them to a construction site somewhere along the waterfront.

The first thing I discovered was that I sweat like a pig. I stopped long enough to take off the nylon windbreaker I'd thrown on over my sweat-shirt. The second thing I discovered was that all the weight-lifting I'd been doing at Psycho's still hadn't prepared me for pedaling. At every hill, I felt the pull on my quadriceps. I found the office building without any trouble, but the construction site was something else. I wandered around for ten minutes before I found out I had the wrong construction gang, and had to go further on up the river. As soon as I'd made the delivery, I went into a sandwich shop and phoned the office.

"Well, if it isn't Richards!" said Benson sarcastically. "Have a nice vacation? I could've *walked* that pickup and delivery and made better time than you did!"

"I had some trouble finding the construction site," I said. "Do you have anything else for me?"

"I'm only doing this because I don't have a replacement yet," Benson said again, and sent me to an airlines office to pick up tickets to deliver to a hotel room. By noon, my body told me I was going to die. If the traffic didn't get me—car drivers that cursed and gave me the finger—my quadriceps would do me in. If not my quadriceps, my heart, my lungs, my liver. . . . At the same time, there was something exhilarating about being out on my own, no one looking over my shoulder. It was up to me to choose my own route, and despite Benson's sarcasm each time I phoned in ("Where you at now, Grandma? Out for a stroll?") he was good at dispatching—never made me backtrack, planned my next pickup as expertly as a traffic controller at the airport.

Forget lunch. I was too keyed up to eat. I drank a Coke while I waited for a security guard at one of the buildings to check out my identification, and it gave me enough energy to get through the day. By midafternoon, in fact, I had learned how to pedal the diagonal streets to beat the grid, and to keep my mouth shut around receptionists who, being lowest on the office totem pole, are looking for someone else to chew out. I learned to dismount and chain my bike almost simultaneously, and to maneuver through city traffic like a cowboy on a horse.

By four-thirty, I think I was running on glands. I kept moving because it took too much effort to stop. I was set on automatic, my brain numb. I made my last run, then phoned the office at four-fifty-nine. Benson sounded half human. "You still aren't ready to quit, Richards?" he asked. "Well, you care to show up here tomorrow, same time, I'll take another five pounds off you."

It was the first intimation I had that the job was mine.

"You want to be called Richards or George?" he went on, "or you got some nickname the friends call you?"

I managed a smile in spite of myself. "Gopher," I told him.

"Gopher? Go-for? Go-far?" His laugh came crackling out of the receiver. "That's a good one. Well, your legs are still working tomorrow, Gopher, I'll see you then."

I was so tired when I got home that I just fell on the couch, legs spread out before me, head tipped over the back. I hadn't even realized that Dad was sitting across the room because the lamp wasn't on. Even when I heard his voice, I was too tired to raise my head.

"How did it go?"

Even my jaws, when I tried to speak, felt sluggish. "Okay, I guess. At least they told me to come back tomorrow."

"The legs hold out okay?"

"Just barely. Oh, man, I'm exhausted!" I felt as though I might fall asleep on the spot—felt one leg jerk the way it does when I'm drifting off. "How's Gramps?" I managed to say.

"Oh, about the same. The doctor says the arterial hemorrhage wasn't too severe or there would have been blood in his spinal fluid, so that's a plus. They've already started physical therapy, but we'll have to wait and see how things shape up. It's his speech that bothers him most. Sometimes he makes sense, and sometimes he doesn't."

"It sure must be hard on Gramps, of all people," I said. Then added, "And on you, too."

Dad was very quiet. I wondered what he was thinking—if he figured that someday it might be him in the hospital and me sitting here, talking with my own son about him. As though we were all moving up a notch in line. Dad sat so still, in fact, that I began to think there was a lecture in the making. It would be the perfect time for him to remind me that Gramps hadn't given me his gold watch just for me to go riding around the streets of Minneapolis on a used Schwinn—that if I felt any respect at all for my grandfather, I would tell him I'd decided to be a credit to the family name after all and go to college.

I heard Dad's chair squeak as he moved, and then the wallpaper turned from gray to rose as Dad flicked on the lamp.

"Mother's still at the hospital with Jeri and Ollie," he said. "You want me to heat up some soup? You're probably starved."

The next few days were both better and worse. Benson blew hot or cold, depending on how much time I saved on deliveries. My muscles hurt worse the second day than they had the first, but by Thursday, I was easily taking hills that had been a real strain before.

One of the things that got to me was simply the noise of the city: the jackhammers, trucks, horns, sirens. A driver yelled at me for not riding close enough to the curb; pedestrians screamed at me for riding too close to them. I began to see everyone in relation to myself: Was that car backing out, purposely trying to cut me off? Was that woman yelling at me? Was that kid thinking of stealing my bike when I parked?

I had to go to a private home in the plush Kensington section of Minneapolis around noon where a woman in a bathrobe gave me some artwork to deliver to a publisher. (So *that's* when they get out of bed in Kensington! I thought.)

The most interesting parts of my day were the elevator rides in office buildings. I figured I must spend a third of my time in elevators. Young women in silk dresses and high heels would get on to stand beside men who had half-drowned themselves in Brut cologne. Standing in the back, of course, unshaven and unshowered, would be me, listening in on their conversations.

It's really weird the way people in suits and silk dresses use the same words over and over again. You hear a lot of "basically" and "in terms of." Lots of "time-frame" or "program." "Let's do lunch, sometime." That's another.

I liked it best when I was alone in an elevator, especially in a tall office building where I could ride all the way to the top. I'd sing a lot when I had an elevator to myself, mostly songs in the Top Forty, theme songs from TV shows or something. Sing at the top of my lungs. The minute the elevator stopped at a floor, of course, I'd clam up.

On Friday, I was in the IDS Tower, all the way to the fifty-third floor, and on the way down, I cut loose with our old school song. Fiftieth floor, forty, thirty, twenty. . . .

The light came on at ninth, and as the elevator stopped, I shut up and resumed my blank look there in one corner. The doors opened. I found myself face to face with Karen Gunderson Ellis.

She didn't move, just stared at me, and then, when the doors started to close, dashed through as I lunged for the "hold" button.

"George!" she said. "My gosh, it's *you!*"

"*Me?*" I croaked. Oh, jeez, *why* hadn't I showered just this once? Why hadn't I at least run the razor over my jaw?

"The one who was singing our school song on the elevator!" she said.

My face must have lit up like a neon sign, and I leaned weakly against the wall. "You . . . you *heard*?"

Karen broke into laughter. "The whole floor could hear! The whole *building!*" Then she said, "No, seriously, just me. Because our office is right across from the elevator, and we keep our door open. The past few days I've been *wondering* who that was, singing in the elevator. And this morning, when I heard our school song, I just had to find out."

"I'll never sing again," I said dolefully.

"Oh, *do!* It makes my day," she said, as the elevator stopped again and more people got on. "Anyway, now that I'm here, I'll ride down to the lobby with you. What are you *doing* here?"

"Minneapolis Messengers," I said. "We've got a regular client on the fifty-third floor." I studied Karen who, if possible, looked even more beautiful than she had before she married, standing there in a pink sweater and gray skirt, high heels—absolutely gorgeous. "What are *you* doing in the building?"

"Putting my husband through college." She smiled. "Actually, we're taking turns. Bob's going full time this year. Then next year, it will be my turn to go and his turn to get a job. Brave new world or something. I just hope it works."

"Sure it will," I told her. "Congratulations again."

"Thanks." She smiled. "Next time you're in the building, stop in on ninth and say hello. Fremont Enterprises."

"What sort of business is it?"

Karen rolled her eyes. "Paper products. Party hats, invitations, paper plates, stationery. . . ." She shrugged. "It's a living."

We'd reached the ground floor, and Karen went on to the mailroom while I went out to my bike. I sniffed under one armpit. I smelled like a goat.

That evening, Ollie and I went to visit Gramps. The nurse had him walking the hall when we got there, and let us take over.

"Good-bye," Gramps said, instead of "Hello," when he saw us, then shook his head in exasperation.

"He gets a little confused when he gets excited, but he's doing just fine," the nurse said.

Gramps was really glad to see us, I could tell, but impatient to go home. Impatient with all the things he couldn't do. His right leg swung stiffly from his hip joint, and although he could move his right arm now, he still found it difficult to pick up objects with his hand. We practiced with him after he sat down, putting things on the tray in front of him so he could try picking them up.

"No damn good," he said after awhile, so we gave up the lesson and told him all the funny things we could think of that had happened to us that day. When I told him the elevator story, he laughed out loud, then suddenly started to cry.

The nurse was standing in the door as we left. "That's not unusual with stroke patients," she said. "Feelings are very close to the surface."

"You think he'll ever be okay again?" Ollie asked as we got in the car.

"See how much he's improved already," I told him.

Ollie didn't say anything for a minute. Then, "Life's short, isn't it?"

It was such a strange remark for a twelve-year-old to make that I looked over at Ollie—at his thin nose and narrow lips, the shock of dark hair on his head. He must have looked just like Dad when Dad was young. "Hey, listen," I said. "Gramps is seventy-three. That's not bad for a life."

"I know, but if *I* only live till seventy-three, that means my life is already . . ." I could see him figuring it out in his head, lips moving, brow furrowed in deep concentration. ". . . one-sixth over. Right, George?"

"With five-sixths yet to go," I commented, trying to put it in perspective. "That's a lot."

"But if one-sixth of my life is already over and I've got to spend the next sixth worrying about Spanish and stuff, and the last sixth will be spent being old, that means I've only got . . . half a life to do what I really want to do."

"Well, maybe you don't have to spend the next sixth worrying about Spanish and stuff." I told him then about Anne, and how she had some pamphlets on forestry. "If that's what you really want to do, Ollie, you'd better start looking into it."

"Dad would kill me," he said.

"Whose life is it, anyway?" I asked him, and we both grinned.

"Yeah," Ollie said. "Maybe I can work for Minneapolis Messengers, too."

He was kidding, of course, but somehow that dig stuck to me all the way home. Even Ollie had me sized up.

Anne hadn't forgotten the brochures. When I picked her up Saturday evening, she handed me an envelope full. "Your brother might like to check out the forest technician jobs," she said. "There's a two-year program in Bemidji, and he *doesn't* have to take Spanish."

We'd planned to go bowling, but after we got to the alley, we just sat out in the car and talked, and then we went uptown for some Chinese food and talked some more. Mostly about Anne, at first. She told me that things were going all right at he Green Thumb, and that Shirl was dating the United Parcel man. *That* was a relief. She also said that when Heather was in the shop the day before, she asked if I still worked there, and when Anne asked why she wanted to know, she said, "Because he's nice."

"Looks like you've got a real fan," Anne said.

"I go over big with eleven year-old girls," I told her.

Little by little, though, the conversation turned to me. I even told Anne that I wanted to be a junior high counselor. Not a doctor, not a lawyer, not an astronaut or anything with initials after my name. Just a counselor. I waited for her to laugh. She didn't bat an eye.

"Then do it," she said. Just what I'd said to Ollie.

I wanted to tell Anne that I really cared about her, but that I had this fantasy girl in the pink sweater at the back of my mind. Tell her we'd met on the elevator that very week, in fact. I felt I should say how I'd taken Maureen Kimball to the prom and spent the evening watching Karen Gunderson, instead. I even wanted to confess that afterwards, on the blanket, it was Karen, not Maureen on my mind. I couldn't, of course, tell her any of it.

Anne was getting up early the next morning to go hiking with friends, so I left her off about eleven and drove home. When I walked in, there was an argument in progress between Dad and Mom and Aunt Sylvia. I went on out in the kitchen to see what I could find, and stood in the pantry eating a slice of roast beef.

"All I'm saying," came Dad's voice, tense, but controlled, "is that somebody has to anticipate Dad's needs for the future. These strokes come without any warning, and the next one could be even worse. I don't see any harm in moving him to a retirement home where there's a nurse on duty, a restaurant where he can buy his meals when he doesn't feel like cooking, and friends his own age, with a full program of activities. If he has a third stroke, there will be people there whose job it is to look in on him regularly."

"But you don't know that *he* wants that," Aunt Sylvia replied. "He's been in the same apartment for eleven years now, ever since Mother died, and it's become home for him. All his furniture is there, and he feels comfortable in it. He's told me many times."

"It's not a question of what he wants; it's a question of what's best for him," Dad boomed.

"Why *isn't* it?" Sylvia shot back. "Why *isn't* it just as important what he wants? And who are we to decide what's best for him?"

"I don't want him alone—to feel that I have to worry about him all the time," Dad answered.

"So it's what *you* want that counts, isn't it?"

I stopped chewing suddenly, surprised at the anger in Aunt Sylvia's voice. It didn't take much for Aunt Sylvia to speak her mind, but it usually took a lot to make her angry. "Phillip, can't you see that you're doing the same thing to Dad that he did to you when you were little? *He* chose the career for you; *he* chose the school. . . . Haven't you forgiven him yet?"

I swallowed.

"That's utter nonsense," said Dad. "I knew I wanted to be a lawyer as far back as fourth grade."

"And Dad knew it the minute you were born. Listen, Phil, one of my earliest memories is Dad carrying you home from the hospital. He walked up on the porch where I was waiting and said, 'Here's your new brother, Sylvia, and some day he's going to be a partner in my firm.' Did you know that?" There was silence from the other room. "When you were only two, Dad used to carry you around on his shoulders and say, 'Make way for the judge; here comes the judge.' "

"It's possible, you know, that he and I wanted the same thing," Dad told her.

"Maybe," said Sylvia. "But right now Dad wants to get back to his apartment in the worst way."

Mom, who had been quiet all this while, said, "There's still another problem, Sylvia. There's a bar association meeting in Chicago later this month. Phil and I were planning to fly down the day after Thanksgiving and have a sort of vacation."

"Well, *go*, by all means!" Sylvia said. "Both Lawrence and I will be here for Thanksgiving, and we'll simply stay over at Dad's apartment with him. You two go have yourselves a great time— you deserve it. But Dad deserves the chance to prove he can stay in that apartment, even if it's a mistake. We're all entitled to make mistakes, Phil. Even you."

I couldn't see Dad from where I was standing, but I tried to imagine him now as a fourth-grader, talking about how he was going to be a lawyer, thinking all the while it was his own decision. *Would* he have been happier doing something else? I didn't know.

And then it came to me that we're all in the same boat. No matter how old and wise you get, you go on making mistakes your whole life: Gramps choosing a career for Dad; Dad trying to push college on his kids; Mom banning me from Dave's house because of his father; Shirley King putting the make on me and Mr. Fletcher too timid to do much about it—all grown-up people who hadn't got the hang of it yet. Somehow I'd thought that when I was an adult, I'd naturally say and do the right thing because I was mature. It wasn't like that. Maybe I'd never make the same mistake of ribbing someone like I did the night Marsh fell in the lake, but I might do something equally foolish later on. There were no guarantees.

It was like homecoming at Thanksgiving, except that Trish and Roger didn't get back. Dave and Discount were both home for the holiday, and I invited the guys over to our place Friday evening.

On Thanksgiving Day itself, though, Uncle Lawrence flew down to be with Aunt Sylvia, and the two of them stayed in the guestroom in Gramps' apartment for the weekend. Gramps, home from the hospital, had put on a red vest for Thanksgiving dinner. He walked slowly, with a limp, and still could not do much with his right hand, but his speech was getting better. There was no question that for now, anyway, he was going to live in his apartment. He let us know that he was the master of his fate, and he'd take the consequences. For much of the meal, in fact, he was his old grumpy self again, complaining that the dressing was too dry, the sweet potatoes too mushy, yet he helped himself to seconds.

We had a good time there at the table. I noticed Dad and me glancing at each other now and then, wondering how the other would react to something we'd said, wanting a good feeling between us again. Several times I caught Mom stopping herself before she made a comment, as though running it first past the censor. It was good, I

183

guess, that we were all trying so hard to get along, but I was looking forward to when we could just be ourselves—act natural. It would still be a while, I guessed.

When Mom and Dad left for Chicago the next day, Mom said to me, "I assume that I can trust the three of you to get along."

"That's asking a lot," I quipped, meaning Jeri and me.

"George, if I thought I had to worry about you. . . ."

"For gosh sake, Mom, go have a good time," I said.

I had to work the Friday after Thanksgiving, of course. I knew that the guys had probably gathered at Psycho's in the afternoon to lift, swap stories; I think that was one of the reasons I'd invited them over that evening. I didn't want to feel left out. Hey, I'm still around, I was saying. Count me in.

Deliveries were slow. A lot of offices didn't even bother to open. I made only two pickups between 8 and 11.

"Stick it out today and you can have tomorrow off," Benson told me when he gave me my next assignment.

Around noon, I found myself in the building where Karen Ellis worked. I had taken to shaving in the mornings and running a stick deodorant around my armpits, so this time I took a chance and stopped on the ninth floor after making my delivery.

The door to Fremont Enterprises was open, and Karen was sitting there at her desk absently munching a sandwich. When she saw me get off the elevator, she swallowed and clapped one hand over her mouth.

"George!" she said, then laughed. "I *knew* if I ate at my desk I'd get caught."

I laughed too and went in.

"The boss is off today," she said, "but guess who had to come in anyway and answer the phone? Sit down. Want half a sandwich?"

"No, I usually get a hot dog later on."

"Oh, *please!* Bob made my lunch this morning and he put in lots! Come on. Ham and swiss, no turkey. It'll go in the waste basket if you don't."

I took half her sandwich and sat there eating it while she talked about the courses Bob was taking at the U. I told her a few of the funny things that had happened to me as a courier, and then my beeper went off. Karen let me use her phone to call Benson, and I got my next assignment.

"I've got a pickup," I told Karen. "Thanks for the lunch. Didn't mean to walk in here and eat yours, though."

"Listen," she said, "drop in any time. I really miss the kids at school. More than I thought I would."

I promised. For the first time, I felt I had been talking to Karen like a friend, not a lover. A rejected lover. A potential lover. Whatever. If you'd asked me six months ago if I could be content being Karen Gunderson's platonic friend, I would have said no way. But there *was* something special about being just friends—not having to worry too much about what you said, or whether the competition was winning. Maybe it was Anne, and how I was beginning to feel about her. Or maybe I was changing in several different ways at once. I don't know.

The guys came over about seven that night bringing one of those six-foot-long submarines on a slab of cardboard wrapped in cellophane.

"Gopher!" they all yelled when I opened the door, and it was as if they hadn't ever been away. We seemed to pick up right where we left off, even though Discount had grown a mustache, Dave was a little fuller about the face, and Psycho actually had a girlfriend. We invited Ollie and Jeri to help eat the sandwich, then both of them went out with friends.

"Jeri," I called when I saw her leaving. "When'll you be home?"

"Two-ish," she said.

"Hey!" I cautioned.

She laughed. "One-ish?"

"Okay," I told her.

"Know what I miss most at school?" Discount said when we'd all sprawled out on the rug and Psycho and I built a fire in the fireplace. "This. Just sitting around gabbing with you guys. You wouldn't *believe* my roommate."

"No matter what he's like, I'll trade you," Dave told him.

"He's into gerbils," said Discount. "I couldn't believe it when I saw him moving them in. It's like a whole gerbil apartment building, with towers and everything. All night long, you can hear the squeak of the damn running wheel."

"I'll take him!" said Dave. "You send him to me parcel post, I'll send you my roommate special delivery, postage paid. He's a jogger."

"So?"

"So you should smell his shoes! He runs without socks. Know what I keep in one corner of our room? A whole bag of charcoal as a deodorizer. It doesn't help. I practically live at the library; can't stand going back to the dorm."

Psycho had a few stories to tell them about the U. of M., and I told about eating lunch with Karen Ellis; but I didn't, strangely, tell them about Anne. Didn't want them asking questions, I guess. Didn't want them seeing her as another Maureen Kimball.

Ollie came in around eleven and went into the den to watch TV. The guys stayed until one-thirty, then left with the understanding that we'd all meet at Dave's the next evening for poker.

I looked in on Ollie. He'd fallen asleep in front of the TV.

"Hey, sport, better get to bed," I said, shaking him gently. I turned off the television and took Ollie by one arm, helping him to his feet. "Jeri happen to tell you where she was going?" I asked.

Ollie stumbled toward the stairs. "Huh uh."

I followed him on up. "She say who she was with?"

He shook his head.

I waited while Ollie took off his shoes. Without bothering to undress, he fell into bed and pulled the covers over him. I shut his door and went back down, closed the screen on the fireplace, and took all the plates and bottles out to the kitchen. One-fifty-seven.

I was upset with Jeri, with Mom, with myself. Mom shouldn't have left without an understanding of who was in charge. I should have insisted on knowing where Jeri would be. If Mom couldn't handle her, how was I supposed to keep her in line while the folks were gone?

I went upstairs, took another shower, and clipped my toenails, just for something to do. Then I sat down with a magazine by the window in my room. But I couldn't read. No matter how I tried to keep my eyes on the page, they traveled to my clock instead. Two-thirty; two-forty-five; two fifty-nine; three. . . .

FIFTEEN

The hour between three and four must have been the most awful hour of my life, unless it was the time we were looking for Psycho in the lake. All the anger I'd been feeling toward Jeri earlier was gone, and in its place there was an almost knee-wobbling kind of fear. I wanted to get in the car and go look for her, but I didn't dare leave the phone. There was little point in calling Aunt Sylvia and Uncle Lawrence, and none at all in calling Mom, who could do nothing from Chicago but worry. At what point does a parent call the police? How long before you file a missing person's report?

I tried to recreate the evening. I remembered inviting Jeri to share the submarine sandwich, and how she'd laughed when she saw it stretched out on the kitchen table. She had taken a small section of it from the middle and sat off on a stool by the refrigerator, listening to the guys kidding around with Dave. I tried to think what she was wearing in case the police should ask. Cords, I thought . . . sort of maroon, maybe, and a white sweater, a lacy knit. Pretty. Jeri wasn't as beautiful as Trish, but she wasn't plain. I remembered the appreciative looks the guys gave her when she walked in the kitchen.

For the seventeenth time, I turned off my lamp and peered down the street, watching for head-lights of an approaching car. By now I had mem-orized every parked car on the street. Should another have driven in while I wasn't watching, I would have spotted it immediately. Nothing.

It was possible, of course, that Jeri was spend-ing the night with a girlfriend and hadn't told me; but the more I clung to the possibility, the more slippery it became. It had been a good evening. Jeri had enjoyed sharing the sandwich with us, pleased to be invited. Any other night, if we were fighting, she'd have delighted in not coming home at all. But tonight, she would have called. I just knew it.

It was five to four and I was standing in the hall outside Ollie's room, deciding whether or not I should ask him to wait by the phone while I went looking, when I heard hurried footsteps on the porch. My heart began to pound wildly. Then the turn of the key in the lock and the soft sound of a door opening and closing.

So why wasn't I overcome with relief? Why didn't all the anger sweep over me again? Why didn't I march downstairs and give Jeri the lecture of her life?

Because there was something different about it. No car had stopped outside, I was sure of it. And then I heard her sob.

I went downstairs. Jeri was standing in the hall-way, leaning against the wall, hugging herself with her arms, coatless. Even in the dim light of the hallway, she looked as though she had been in a whirlwind. Her hair was in tangles about her face and shoulders, her cheeks flaming red from the wind. Her hands stood out chapped and red against her sweater. She knew I was there, but she went on crying. I was almost afraid to ask. The fear returned.

"Jeri," I said finally, "I was worried." I couldn't think of anything better. What do you say when you expect the worst? What would Mom have said, I wondered, when whatever you say might be wrong?

Jeri turned her face even further toward the wall until her forehead touched the plaster and her shoulders shook. There were ugly bruises on her cheek and around one eye.

The only time in my life I could remember putting my arms around my sister was once for a family portrait, but this time it came automatically, if only to warm her. And suddenly she fell against me, her fists against my chest, the tears soaking into my shirt. Only her tears were warm. She was shivering as though she couldn't stop.

"Tell me what happened," I said, and led her into the living room. I sat her down on the sofa and got two ski jackets from the closet, tucking them in around her. I could hear her teeth chattering. "Who were you with?"

"G . . . Gus," she said, and sobbed again.

I waited. "Somebody from school?"

"No."

"From the 18-20 Club? The marine?"

"No. S . . . somebody else. You don't know him." She sniffled.

"Where's your coat?"

"B . . . back at his place." Her voice suddenly

became high and mouselike. "He wouldn't *give* it to me, George! He wouldn't let me g . . . go! He . . . he *hit* me!"

I sat down beside her and put her hands in mine, rubbing warmth back into them. They felt like slivers of ice. Slowly, in bits and pieces, the story came out. She had been dating Gus for a couple of months. He was one of the most popular males at the 18-20 Club, and twice he'd come out tops on the ballot. He was nineteen, Jeri said, and she didn't have to tell me what a thrill it was, when you're sixteen, to have an older guy pay attention to you. Had she made it with him? I asked. No, Jeri said, but he was insisting. The tears came again.

"He wouldn't *listen,* George! He was crazy! So I left."

"This was at his place?" I asked.

She nodded, pulling one hand away to wipe her eyes, then quickly edged it back into my own hands again. It still felt cold between my palms. "His parents are away for the weekend."

"Maybe everybody's gone to Chicago for the Bar Association meeting," I said, trying to lighten things up. Jeri smiled weakly, but her lips trembled. "So what'd you do, Jeri? Walk home?"

"Yes."

"Where does he live?"

"Over near the airport."

"Ye gods, that's at least three miles!"

Jeri pressed her lips together. More tears. "I'm through with him," she said.

I kept one hand over Jeri's and leaned back, stretching my other arm along the back of the couch. We sat there quietly for a while. I was thinking how, for the last ten years, Jeri and I could hardly be in a room two minutes together without bickering.

"Jeri," I said finally, "is this your style? Going home with guys?"

"No!" There was a trace of indignation in her voice. "The only other time I did something like this was when I went to a motel with somebody from school and absolutely nothing happened."

"You went to a motel with somebody and nothing happened?"

"It was a dare," Jeri said. "Somebody bet we wouldn't go." She took her hand away and folded her arms across her chest. "Okay, get it over with. The lecture."

"No lecture," I told her. "Just trying to figure you out. I've heard you sneaking in late . . . going out after we thought you were in for the night."

"Well, nothing happened those times either, not really," Jeri said, and her voice was small again. "I suppose . . . I'm just so . . . totally sick of people thinking of me as, you know, Jeri the Brain."

I realized then that the things I had disliked the most about Jeri in the past were actually the same things I saw in myself. We both wanted to be independent, which was fine, but we carried it to the point of near-lunacy.

"So will the real Jeri Richards please stand up?" I joked.

Jeri gave me a sidelong look. "What's with you, anyway?"

"We're pretty much alike," I told her. "Whatever the folks want us to do, we do the opposite. Some day, if they say 'breathe,' we're going to stop breathing just to spite them."

"Look who's talking."

"Exactly!"

Jeri sighed. "How am I going to get my coat back?" she asked finally.

"Leave that one to me," I told her.

I didn't sleep much the rest of the night, and at seven I called the guys.

"Do you know what *time* it is?" each of them bawled.

I said that Jeri's ex roughed her up and we had to pay him a visit right then, while he was still home. "The Hell's Angels look," I told them.

They grumped, but they came. They gave up five more hours of sleep and drove over. Discount arrived in his Dad's leather hunting jacket; Dave was wearing a motorcycle helmet and a bike chain wrapped around his knuckles; and Psycho, all 185 pounds of him, simply wore his football jersey with a T-shirt over it saying "Search and Destroy."

Jeri had given me Gus Lindstrom's name before she'd gone off to bed, and I'd looked up the address in the phone book. We pulled up outside his house at a quarter of eight, and we all clomped up on the porch, making as much noise as possible, spitting out the sides of our mouths.

I figured he'd still be sleeping. I rang the doorbell seven or eight times, then I used the knocker. Between the fourth and fifth barrage, I thought I heard faint footsteps from inside. Then it was quiet, but I could tell, the way you sort of know, that the guy was looking at us through a side window.

"Hey, Gus, open up!" I called.

The silence from inside went on.

"Might be able to go in through a window," I said loudly.

"Kick in the back door," huffed Dave, and it was all I could do not to laugh.

Psycho nodded to Discount, and the two of them lumbered around to the back and began pounding on the door.

Obviously, Jeri's ex must have felt the house was under seige, because all at once a window above us opened and Gus stuck his head out. He was awake, let me tell you.

"What do you want?" he called.

"My sister's coat, pal," I told him.

He studied me for a moment. "You her brother?"

"Would I be here if I wasn't?"

He still hesitated. Around in back, Psycho began banging on the door again, rattling the windows.

"Okay, just a minute," Gus said. A moment later he leaned out the window again with Jeri's coat and dropped it down.

"You going to let us in?" I asked, knowing he'd throw himself in front of a tractor-trailer before he opened the door.

"Why should I?"

"Want to have a little talk."

"I don't have a thing to say to you," he answered.

"Well, I got a message from Jeri," I told him as Psycho and Discount came around from in back and we all stood together there on the steps, the Killer Quartette. "She's through with you, Gus. You don't want to see us again, you don't see her. Understood?"

Gus didn't answer.

"You lay a hand on her again, you'll need a shovel to pick yourself up. You got it?"

He got it. Gus pulled his head back in so fast that he bumped it on the window.

We hung around a little longer. Bud chinned himself a few times on a branch of the maple there in the yard, while Psycho merely picked up the fence gate and, holding it above his head, went up on the porch and deposited it against the front door. We swaggered back to the car finally, Dave rewinding the bicycle chain around his fist, and as we climbed in, I knew that Gus had his eyes on us all the way.

On Monday, after the guys had gone back to school, I made my first pickup and delivery, then called the admissions office at the U. I told them I'd been accepted for the fall quarter, but had turned it down.

"I'd like another chance," I said. "What do I do now?"

They said my application was still on file, but I'd need to come in and update it. Registration was closed for the winter term, but they could put my name on the waiting list. There was a chance. . . .

I hadn't expected, actually, that I'd even be considered till next fall, so I wasn't disappointed. I had a job, and being a bicycle messenger in three feet of snow would be an experience. The main thing was, when I went to college, I'd be going because *I* wanted to be there, which is the only reason to go at all.

I called Anne that night and told her that she might find me in one of her classes come spring.

"I think I could stand that," she said.

There hadn't been any enormous change in our family, but the invisible walls had come down at the table and we were communicating far beyond the "Pass the butter" stage. We even joked now and then. Dad was telling one night about a road sign he'd seen: DEMOCRACY BOULEVARD; LEFT TURN ONLY. And of course that got us going. Mom's contribution was a sign near a highway that was being repaired that read LOOSE JOINTS. And then I remembered the one we'd seen on our trip to the ocean, around Nags Head: LEAVE SHIP-WRECKS FOR OTHERS TO ENJOY. I liked making the family laugh, getting a smile out of Dad.

The most dramatic change, I guess, was that Jeri and I weren't enemies anymore. Probably no one else in the family noticed. It was just a feeling between us, but it was there.

I hadn't planned to tell the folks about calling the admissions office at the U. I figured that when the call came and there was an opening, I'd tell them then.

Friday evening, however, as Mom put the roast on the table, she said, "George, your Dad and I are thinking about Christmas gifts this year, and we decided we'd better tell you in advance so you can pick yours out. I'm sure you'd rather choose it yourself."

I looked up.

Dad was cutting his meat, eyes on his plate:

"I've just been noticing," he said, "how the couriers who come to our office ride those European bikes that probably make twice the time that Schwinn you're using does. If you want, you can choose a new bike—any model you like."

To anyone else looking in on our family, this would have been ordinary dinner conversation, but what Dad was saying was more difficult for him than you'd have thought. He wasn't just offering me a gift; he was offering acceptance of the way I was.

For a moment I wasn't sure how to answer. Letting them back into my life wasn't easy for me either, but Dad had come halfway.

"It'd be nice," I said, "but there's a chance I'll be going to the University next quarter. It's only a chance, but if not then, probably spring. So I guess I can make do with the Schwinn until then."

Mom's eyes lit up, and she put down her fork. She and Dad exchanged pleased but wary glances. I could tell they were trying to choose their words carefully, trying hard not to say the wrong thing. I wanted to make it easier for them.

"I've finally decided what I want to do," I said. "It probably won't take more than a master's degree, and I'll never make a lot of money at it, but I'd sort of like to go into counseling. School counseling, I mean."

I realized when I said it that not even Jeri and Ollie were in on it yet. Any other time, Jeri would have brayed, "You!! A counselor!!" She didn't.

Mom was obviously happy about it. I had actually said those magic words—college—master's degree—but she knew I was going for myself, not for her.

"I think you'll make a fine counselor," she said, and went on smiling as she buttered her roll.

It was Dad's reaction, though, that was important somehow. Obviously, he wasn't jumping up and down with joy. I hadn't said law school. I hadn't said medicine. I hadn't said Harvard, Princeton, or Yale. Whatever it was he was planning to say right then, however, didn't get said, because suddenly Ollie got up his nerve and sailed in on my coattails:

"I know what *I* want to do, too!" he said. "I want to be a forest technician, and I'm going to a special school in Bemidji after I graduate from high school. I've got all sorts of papers on it, what courses I have to take and everything."

"A forest technician?" Dad said, frankly staring.

"It's a two-year program. It's like an assistant to a forest ranger, but you get to do all kinds of different stuff," Ollie told him.

A school counselor and an assistant to a forest ranger. I began to wonder just how much a man's nervous system could take at one time.

Dad looked at Ollie and me as though words escaped him. Then he picked up his fork again and went on cutting his meat. "Well," he said at last, "the most marvelous thing about the human organism is its ability to change."

Uh-oh, I thought. Here it comes. How you can always switch your major after you discover you're in the wrong field. How you can go your first two years of college at one school and then transfer over to one with a "reputation." How Ollie and I would eventually come to our senses. But it wasn't Ollie and me that Dad was talking about.

"Maybe we've got enough lawyers in this family," he told us. "There's something to be said for surprises, I guess." He was smiling just a bit. It was still the strained smile, a little forced, but it looked as though the wires had slackened somewhat, and that, with practice, a real smile would work its way through. "When will you know?" he asked me. "About the University?"

"In a few weeks," I told him. "If I don't get in the winter quarter, I've still got my job."

When dinner was over, Jeri and I helped Mom carry dishes to the kitchen. Jeri plopped the bread basket on the counter and said, "Well, I'm beginning to sound like the weirdo around here, but *I* still want to go to Radcliffe. Maybe *I'll* end up being a lawyer!"

She and Mom looked at each other for a moment, and then they both started to laugh. "Well . . . *why not?*" said Mom, and handed the silverware to me.

I took Ollie over to Psycho's later to work out. The air had a heavy moist feel to it. I turned the collar up on my jacket. Typhus trotted along beside us.

"Snow, I'll bet," I said. "Guess I'll have a chance to see what the Schwinn can do in that."

"I want to be a forest technician where there's snow," Ollie said. "You learn about all kinds of animal paw prints and where to put out food in the winter. That's the part I'd like best. You think I'll make it, George? The two-year program? There's some pretty hard stuff in those courses. I've been reading about them."

"Hey listen, Ollie," I told him, "you're one out

of four hundred million, you know that? Four hundred million spermatazoa . . . ."

"What?"

"Spermatazoa. Sperms."

"Oh."

"Four hundred million spermatazoa were racing for the ovum when you were conceived, and you're the sperm that got there first. There must have been something pretty special about the one that made it."

In the dim glow of the streetlight, I could see Ollie peering over at me, his dark eyes looking out from under the hood of his sweat jacket. He didn't say a word, but a smile was spreading slowly across his face. He gave an awkward leap there on the sidewalk, grasping for a twig high overhead, and then, still smiling, climbed on up the hill toward Psycho's.